LOCKED on LOVE'S LANDING

D. E. MALONE

Locked on Love's Landing
Copyright © 2025 D.E. Malone
All rights reserved.
Cover designed by Red Leaf Book Design
Library of Congress Cataloging-in-Publication Data has been applied for

For exclusive content and book news, subscribe to D.E. Malone's *Welcome to the Sweet Life* newsletter.

Also by D.E. Malone

Chapter One

I f she chose a motto to live by, Kit Wendell swore by the words on a poster that had hung in her high school science lab twenty years ago:

Perseverance Paves the Way to Success.

But perseverance was decidedly not paving the way at the moment.

In fact, she'd skinned a finger with the hand drill while trying to repair a ladder rung on the *Dolly Swain*, her freshly repainted tug-turned-passenger-ferry, in time for today's tour. The rustle of leaves skittering across the walking path and the sublime sound of water lapping against the boat's hull did little to soothe her frayed patience and the chiding of her oldest sister, Rose.

"Are you sure you shouldn't call someone to help you with that?" Rose's tone suggested Kit should drop the drill and get on the phone now. She stood over Kit, casting a shadow over Kit's work area.

Kit caught the screw that popped out of the hole before it fell into the water. "I don't need to pay someone to do some-

1

thing I can very easily do for myself. People call *me* to help with this kind of stuff."

"The 'easily' part appears to be a stretch," Rose said.

She twisted around where she knelt, shielding her eyes from the sun as she looked up at Rose.

"Look, thank you for bringing the donuts, but your commentary isn't helping."

Rose stood by with an armload of pastry boxes filled with her Apple Hill Farm's signature cider donuts. If Kit's finger wasn't bleeding and the rung was in place, she would have taken the boxes from Rose so her sister could be on her way back to the farm.

That perseverance thing sometimes acted like a curse.

Kit flipped her braid over her shoulder again as she fixed her concentration on the ladder. Setting her jaw, she pushed on the ladder's base section again, so the gap between it and the rung closed for the umpteenth time. Then she braced her knee against the cold metal to hold the two disconnected pieces in place.

Quickly, before it shifted, she set the screw. The drill whined as the threads disappeared until the screw head was flush with the step.

She shook the ladder to test its strength. Placed a foot on the rung. Gave it a little bounce.

Solid. *There*.

Rose let out a loud sigh. "Where can I put these? I need to get back to the farm."

"On the bench behind you, please."

She pointed with her elbow to the bench alongside the walking path. Her group would meet there for donuts and coffee before climbing aboard for the ride. She'd already picked up the thermoses from Coffee Loft in downtown Greenhaven. Her friend and Coffee Loft owner, Ginger Giatti, had the coffee ready to go an hour ago when Kit arrived at the shop.

"Okay, see you. Hope your day gets better," Rose said.

"Wait." Kit set the drill on the ground and hurried over to give Rose a parting hug. "Sorry for being surly."

Rose rubbed a circle on her back, just like Mom did. It made her smile. They were so much alike. Always coming through in a heartbeat.

"No worries. Happy to help," Rose said, pulling away.

"Tell Trav I'm looking forward to him acting as my first mate on Saturday."

Rose chuckled as she backed away, swinging the arm of the sweatshirt she'd tied around her waist. "He hasn't stopped talking about it."

"I'm sure the ladies will love him, too."

Rose's twelve-year-old son, Travis, had been pestering Kit for months to give him the official title and a chance to help during one of her tours. The perfect opportunity presented itself last month when Mona Jarvis, mayor of Port Chance, booked a tour for her mother's eightieth birthday. Mona, her mother, and seven friends would spend the morning sipping mocktails and sampling breakfast pastries from Apple Hill Farm's bakery. She'd keep Travis busy with tending to their needs while she navigated them up the river to Dubuque and back.

Rose walked into the parking lot and got into the farm truck. The engine rumbled to life before the noise faded as Rose drove away from Love's Landing.

Kit disassembled the drill and tucked it and the other tools she'd scattered on the dock into her tool box before hoisting it

3

over the ladder and onto the deck. She hopped aboard, then grabbed the small folding table and a duffle of supplies that Rose collected for her. She'd convinced Kit that the pre-tour gatherings were a ripe opportunity to make a good first impression.

You have to look like you care about giving guests the full experience instead of just a boat ride, Rose had said.

Kit thought her clients were paying for an experience on the river, not a table with fancy accoutrements like overpriced napkins and molded plastic cups trying to pass as crystal. But Rose was the brand master behind making Apple Hill Farm the go-to destination in the Quad Cities. If she thought Kit's new business venture could benefit from fancy picnic ware, who was she to argue?

She climbed down the ladder, set the table and bag at her feet, then tested the rung one last time with a few bounces. It held fast.

"Hey there, Kitty Kat."

Confusion made her freeze.

She hadn't heard that nickname since her youth. But the voice? Its teasing drawl mixed with the deep, masculine tone she'd heard all too recently—at Will Alexander's wedding a few months ago to be exact. She'd hoped it would be a single occurrence, never to be repeated. Holden Berne left Port Chance years ago, leaving her broken heart in his wake. He didn't belong here anymore. In Port Chance, and especially not standing on her dock.

When she stepped off the ladder and turned, Holden, all six-foot-something of him, braced himself on the rocking pier with a wide-legged stance. His grin broadened now that he had her attention.

"Bet you haven't heard that in a while," he quipped.

A gusty breeze pushed an ample amount of dark hair over his forehead. With a shadow beard tracing his jawline, Holden was barely recognizable as the lanky version of his younger self. The surprise at seeing him slowly ebbed. In its place, the old feelings of longing and defensiveness crept up. Kit steeled herself against both.

"Not since I reached maturity. Guess that means you haven't?" She crossed her arms as she tapped her bare foot, which felt less intimidating without her shoes.

He snorted. "Still slinging insults as deftly as you threw a ball, I see."

She lifted a shoulder, looking out across the water. She'd been less surprised to see him at the wedding than she was now. People who had left Port Chance behind sometimes popped up again for one reason or another. Like at weddings or homecoming games. But on her dock?

"It's a gift I don't take for granted."

Holden smiled and shook his head as he stepped closer. This time the breeze caught the citrus scent mingling with the woodsy base of his cologne, and she wrinkled her nose. Not only did he look older, he even smelled different. *Good* different.

"We didn't get to catch up at the wedding," he said.

Not sorry about that. "It was a busy night."

"It was." He shrugged. "But, here I am."

"You're here to catch up *now*? The wedding was months ago."

"Better late than never," he said as he pulled his hands out of his pockets and turned his palms up in apology. "It's been a busy summer."

"Exactly. And a busy fall, so I'd better get back to work if you don't mind." It was so like him to come and go as he pleased, expecting his desires to fall into place when convenient.

"Busy night. Busy fall. I'm getting a hint of a hint here," he said with another flash of a smile.

"You're quick to catch on."

His expressive brows, which had always displayed his every emotion, pulled together.

"Seriously, now. Let's cut the banter, Kit. I can come back another time, but I really want to find out what you're up to these days."

She took a step back with a firm shake of her head. "There's really no reason for that—

"Kit, I wouldn't do that." He reached for her even though she wasn't close enough to grasp.

"You have a lot of— *WHOA!*"

Holden's eyes bugged out as her foot found nothing but air when she took another step back. Her arms pinwheeled for a desperate second before her other foot lost contact with the dock, and she toppled over backward into the water.

Coldcoldcoldcold

Seconds after hitting the water, her heels sank into the silty river bottom.

The shock of falling had barely registered before a tidal wave of water was displaced beside her and a pair of gorilla arms wrapped around her middle, tugging her toward the reedy bank. She sputtered and spit out a mouthful of swampy river water.

Gripping vegetation to pull herself up the bank, she finally got her feet underneath her. Behind her, Holden was having less luck gaining his footing. Cobbles tumbled into the water as he pulled himself out of the river, grunting with the effort.

She looked down at herself, drenched to the bone. Her group would arrive within a half hour, and she looked like a wet rat. All this happened because he couldn't take a hint.

Nothing's changed.

"Are you alright?" he asked when he stood, taking a fistful of his long-sleeved polo to wring the water from it. He wasn't even looking at her, more concerned with his appearance than her. His sodden shoes made sucking sounds with each step as he walked toward her.

"No, I'm far from all right!" She brushed futilely at her water-logged clothes.

He puffed out his chest. "Look on the bright side. If I hadn't saved you, you might be in worse shape," he said with a cheerful note.

"*Saved* me? The water is waist high."

He stopped balling the fabric in his fists.

"People can drown in a cupful of water," he added.

She shook with irritation, but also from the unexpected bath. The air temperature was near seventy degrees, but the breeze made her teeth chatter.

"Listen, I have a tour group coming soon, and I get to welcome them aboard like this, thanks to you." She grabbed the hem of her wet shirt with the Muddy Bottom Tours logo emblazoned across the front and peeled it over her head, tossing it against his chest with a wet thud. "Great first impression. Thanks."

She was too mad to worry about discretion, or the fact that Holden stared at her, mouth agape, while she stood there in a tank top which left little to the imagination. Just like old times, his presence threw her completely off kilter, to the point she'd walked backward off her own dock, and he barely seemed to notice.

Holden's interest in her attire turned to frustration. "I'm sorry, but you were the one—"

She pointed a finger at him to shut him up. "Don't even turn this back on me."

"But if you weren't so hostile to begin with—"

She stomped over to the boat and pulled herself aboard to find her wallet.

Why did Holden care to save her in the first place? She'd spent almost two decades reconciling the fact that he'd left town without a word. Seeing him after all this time brought all the hurt rushing back. She didn't want to think about this now, yet what choice did she have?

"This is how you're going to make it up to me," she called over her shoulder, fishing out some cash, then hopped off the boat again. She walked up to Holden and pressed the bills against his chest.

"You're going to go to Happy Heart Collective right now and bring me back a pair of pants and a sweatshirt as fast as you can. Got it?"

He glanced down at the twenties she held against him as if his brain was slow to connect the dots. "Happy Heart Collective?"

"That's what I said." *Did the river seep into his brain? Why does he look so dazed?*

"All right," he drawled finally.

"Size eight, medium. It's a few doors down from the church." She tossed him a towel she'd grabbed from a compartment underneath the padded benches on the boat. "You'll need this."

Holden stared at the towel as if he'd never seen one before.

"*Now*, please." She snapped her fingers a few times to hurry him along. Anything to make him disappear so she could collect her thoughts. There was also the real possibility that her heart— *her traitorous heart!* —might leap from her chest to flop around on the dock like a beached fish. *Holy bells, did he look good.*

He jumped and ran-walked across the dock, down the sidewalk, and hopped the curb to cross the street, leaving a thin trail of water behind him.

She twisted the single braid that dripped over her shoulder like a leaky hose. A puddle gathered around her feet. Thank goodness she'd kicked off her shoes and left them on the deck, or he'd be buying her shoes, too.

Holden.

What compelled him to come back to annoy her after all this time? She smiled despite the bad timing and the water content of what little she wore now. He was just as drenched as she was, yet she'd sent him shopping.

Still feeling every micro beat of her pulse, she nodded decisively to his retreating figure across the street.

Serves him right.

Chapter Two

A few minutes later, Holden rushed into Happy Heart Collective, out of breath and flustered. He kicked off his water-soaked shoes next to the door and padded barefoot to the nearest rack of clothes. Several women stopped sifting through the clothes nearby to stare.

Shop for Kit? Twenty years ago, maybe, but this woman was a stranger now.

Woman.

So strange to think of Kitty Kat as a woman. But, man, she sure looked the part.

A chuckle brewed in his chest. She'd practically jumped out of her skin when he'd used her nickname. It wasn't the sweet trip down memory lane he'd intended. Not at all. Instead, the eye-popping, red-faced reaction she delivered surprised him. But she'd always been feisty. That's one of the things he'd loved about her.

"Can I help you with something?"

A silver-haired clerk, who looked vaguely familiar, approached, probably wondering if he'd made a wrong turn into the shop. His wet clothes hung on him but, thankfully, he'd stopped dripping on the way here after peeling off his shirt in the alley and giving it a good wringing out. He'd draped Kit's towel around his waist like a skirt over his jeans.

"I need pants and a sweatshirt, size eight." His heart beat like a jackhammer. It couldn't be that he was out of shape; he worked out religiously. *Blame it on Kit.*

"For?" She looked him up and down as she tried to picture him filling those dimensions. Her gaze settled on his face, and she lit up. "Wait. *Holden Berne?*"

"That's me." A hazy memory of her sitting at a round table in the basement of Good Shepherd Methodist Church rushed forward. Hazel, that was her name. A church friend of his grandparents.

"How is Joelle?" she asked. "I haven't seen her in ages."

"She's still as salty as ever. She and my grandfather are in assisted living near Hannibal." He glanced toward the window even though Love's Landing wasn't visible from Main Street. Kit was probably turning inside out with impatience.

"And your parents? They're still near there, too?"

"Yes, ma'am."

She clasped her hands together, looking up at the tin ceiling with a shake of her head. "I sure do miss them. I wish they hadn't moved away."

"I'll tell them you said 'hello.'"

"I'd love that. Tell them anytime they want to visit, I've got a spare bedroom waiting for a guest or two." She dropped her hands and scanned him from head to toe again.

"I'm sorry, but we don't carry men's clothes, though you look like you desperately need some," she said with a half-smile.

"I'm not worried about myself at the moment. They're for someone else."

She led him to a rack of medium-sized sweatshirts. "Who are you shopping for? Picking something up for Joelle? A girlfriend?"

"Just a friend. Kit Wendell." Of course she knew Kit. It was a small town, after all. The Wendells were one of those Port Chance families who had been around for generations.

"You're shopping for Kit?" she said in disbelief. Her hand fluttered to her cheek as if she feared for his life. "You're very *brave*."

"I am. I'm also in a bit of a rush."

He needed to find something like *now*, and he didn't want to dwell on the *who* part, or what led to this awkward mission in the first place. He snatched the first shirt he spotted in the medium section and held it up. *Right size. Perfect.*

"I'll take this."

Hazel didn't try to disguise her skepticism. "If you're sure..."

"It'll do." He prayed it'd work.

The drab gold sweatshirt looked similar to the Bedden High School Hornets colors, except for the strange-looking, cartoonish pickle on the front wearing a cowboy hat.

Beggars can't be choosers.

Kit always had a sense of humor anyway. At least she used to.

Hazel finally got the hint that he was in a hurry when she plucked a pair of gray pants with a rhinestone pocket design from another rack.

"Too fancy," he said, shuffling through the selection himself, wishing he'd noticed what she was wearing before that tank top made its appearance. "Here. These will work." The tan canvas pants looked plain enough for Kit. She'd never been into embellishments from what he remembered.

At the front counter, Hazel calculated the total. "Our return policy—"

"These won't be returned." He planned to give Kit back her money and cover the expense himself. It was *his* fault anyway, according to Kit.

Again, Hazel looked unsure, judging by the downward turn of her mouth.

"Nice to see you again, Holden." She handed him the plastic bag across the counter. "Don't be a stranger."

Kit was floating a tablecloth over a folding table when he hurried back to Love's Landing. She'd also cocooned herself in a parka to cover that wet tank top, thank goodness. The memory of her peeling off her soaked shirt would live in his memory until his dying day.

"You bought me a Port Chance *Pickles* sweatshirt?" she wheezed when she held it at arm's length a few seconds later.

"You didn't tell me not to. In fact, the only criteria I shopped with was a medium sweatshirt."

"This was a satire team years ago," Kit said with an exaggerated sour look. "One to commemorate the worst losing record of any high school baseball team in the school's history."

He frowned. He'd played baseball. His team hadn't exactly had stellar years, but he remembered winning on occasion.

"Sorry, that's all they had." *Gosh, she's pretty, even when she's drenched.*

"I hoped for something a little less...ostentatious. I'll be a laughingstock." She dropped her arms to give him a hard look.

Her fresh-faced beauty, despite the frown, triggered a hitch in his throat when he swallowed.

"Think of it as a conversation starter."

"Or the one thing that loses me a rec." She crumpled the clothes into her arms. "Anyway, thanks, I guess. I need to change. My group will be here soon."

"So, how about we get together for coffee, or— Hey, do you still like coconut cream pie?" They'd spent many days after school eating at Daisy Gap Café. Her older sister Janie had waitressed there, too.

"Gave up pie years ago," she said flatly.

"Oh."

Kit had also spent summer afternoons sitting at his Nana's dining room table, digging into strawberry rhubarb pie, his grandmother's specialty. Now she claimed to be off the pie wagon. He didn't believe her.

"Coffee, too," she added.

She wore that defiant, chin-up look that he knew too well. There would be no concessions today.

"Interesting."

She looked over his shoulder. "My tour group is here. I need to go."

He watched her pull herself up the ladder and disappear into the cabin. Several vehicles had wheeled into the parking spaces on the other side of the walk.

Not if I see you first.

He'd make sure of it.

* * *

Holden pulled into a gas station before he left Port Chance to change into the dry sweatpants he'd found in the gym bag in his car. Then he headed into the office at EcoPartners in downtown Greenhaven to retrieve his laptop. Portia, his assistant, would fire questions at him as soon as he walked in the door—he'd bet on it. With an eagle eye for detail—that's why he'd hired her, after all—she'd notice right away that he'd changed at some point between leaving the office that morning and returning now. One more clean pair of pants and a shirt should be in his suitcase back at the hotel before he needed to do laundry. His new rental would be move-in ready by Monday, Portia assured him, and it came with a washer and dryer.

As soon as he walked into his second-floor office, Portia was onto him.

"What happened to you?" She stood up from her desk to peer at him from head to toe.

"Had an unplanned date with the river," he mumbled.

She crossed her arms. "I think there's more to the story than that. What aren't you telling me?"

"I ran into an old friend. She wasn't exactly happy to see me."

"Then I don't think 'friend' is the right word to use."

"You're probably right." He shook his head, sitting down in his office chair to ditch his sodden shoes.

"Holden, here. Let me get you a towel, or your shirt's going to soak that chair. Then you'll never get the river smell out of it."

Portia was right. He stood, giving the seat a half-hearted brush with his fingertips.

His assistant scurried into one of the empty offices and came out with two large towels.

"Thank you. Did the governor's office return my call?" He rubbed his head with one of the towels.

"Not yet. But Dan did," she said, returning to her desk. "He said he'll make the day work whenever the governor schedules a date. He also said he'd pop in sometime this afternoon."

"Good ol' Dan. Can always count on him."

He'd met his buddy, Dan Brieze, in basic training at Fort Leonard Wood. They'd been deployed together to the Middle East for eight months, then when their service commitment was up a year later, they'd attended the same college together. Dan had helped Holden land an entry-level job at the Army Corps of Engineers office in Quincy. They'd worked together for several years before Holden moved on to start EcoPartners.

After he packed his laptop, Holden jotted down some notes. He checked the time, knowing it would be too late to head back to Port Chance when Dan arrived today. They'd do a recon of the river tomorrow to get the scope of the clean-up project. Dan would coordinate the volunteer force with Portia's help. Holden had been trying to entice him to give up the life of a public servant and come work for him. So far, the government pension was too attractive for Dan to leave.

"What days are available for the tour?" Portia's fingers were poised above her keyboard ready to input the date into the calendar once she handed off the towels and sat at her desk again.

"I didn't get that far."

Her fingers curled before she looked up again.

"I know. I failed."

"What do you mean? Isn't that the reason you paid this Katherine Wendell person a visit? To talk about a possible schedule?"

"Yes, but...like I said, it didn't go well." He sighed loudly, letting Portia know the emotional toll his visit with Kit had taken on him. "I'll give you her number."

"This sounds like unfinished business that needs to be sorted out by you, not me," Portia said.

"You know I have trouble with confrontations. Scheduling a tour is business, and not a personal issue anyway."

Portia snorted. "I've seen her website. Katherine Wendell, owner of Muddy Bottom Tours, is easy to look at."

"Her name's Kit." She'd insisted everyone call her Kit in junior high, which was when he'd started calling her Kitty Kat. Man, had she hated that.

"Katherine, Kit, whatever. I'll schedule the tour, but you need to get your behind back over there and fix things before we take this tour," she said, while her fingers flew over the keyboard. "Personal drama won't look good in front of the governor, you know. Not if you want her signing legislation."

Yes, he did know.

But he hadn't imagined himself and Kit taking a plunge in the Mississippi when he got the crazy idea to hire her for a shoreline tour with the governor and a few well-connected constituents. Nor did he expect the chip on her shoulder to still be present when he saw her again after their initial run-in at Will Alexander's wedding this past spring. And the incident on Love's Landing happened almost twenty years ago. He'd let it go. Why couldn't she?

But no, this was Kit. It shouldn't surprise him.

Portia was right, though. He wasn't about to let a Kit-sized grudge keep him from getting on her schedule. It was nothing a little phone call wouldn't solve. Maybe he'd send over an apology pie, too. He'd never buy what Kit said about giving it up.

And he'd happily risk a fall in the river again to find out.

Chapter Three

Kit pulled her truck into her sister Rose's driveway at Apple Hill Farm, parking it under the red maple near their house. The engine shuddered and hitched to a stop when she switched off the ignition. That camshaft needed to be replaced, like, yesterday. It wasn't a cheap repair, but that wasn't the issue. It was time, or her lack of it. She should have brought her car instead, giving the old girl a break.

Patting the dash for encouragement, she opened her door and landed on two feet to face the menagerie roaring down the drive as soon as they spotted her.

Balzac, the family's Saint Bernard mix, buried his head into her stomach as she braced herself for his bulk. Behind him, Travis and his twin brothers ran down from the main barn to meet her, too. She'd waited until the farm closed to customers before coming, since fighting traffic at the apple farm, especially during harvest season, was not something she needed at the end of a work day. Besides, she'd headed home first to change out of the ridiculous Port Chance Pickles sweatshirt. Rose and Jordan had invited her to dinner, along with the rest of the family, and that would surely have drawn unwanted questions.

"Aunt Kit, look what we found by the big barn," called six-year-old Alex as they approached her. He cradled something in his cupped hands.

Kit closed the door, pushing Balzac's immense head out of the way to save his snout, and peered into Alex's hands.

"A pinkie squirrel? You didn't find any others?"

Aaron, Alex's twin, shook his head. "Only one. No nests around. Hawk probably dropped it."

"Poor thing. Is Sadie here yet? She'll know what to do."

Sadie, the third oldest of the four Wendell sisters, was a wildlife rehabber, a job so fitting for her she could have founded the cause. She voluntarily took in sick and injured wild animals to care for, relying on donations and grants to cover expenses. Luckily, her remote work as a customer service rep for a state utility company allowed her flexibility and a chance to work from home.

"There she is," Travis said, pointing. The twins took off to meet Sadie's little red economy car coming up the long gravel drive.

"Are you excited about being my first mate on Saturday?" She ruffled Travis's mop of hair. "I'll sure need the help."

"Mom said they're all, like, *eighty years old*?" His eyes bugged out.

"That's what I hear. They'll be a rough bunch. Sure you can handle it?"

Travis nodded slowly, looking a little nervous.

"They'll love you. No worries, Trav."

Kit chuckled to herself as he trotted off to join his brothers. They mobbed Sadie as her sister stepped out of her car. Sadie took the rambunctious boys in humorous stride, but Kit knew their energy levels drained her introverted sister after too long.

Aromas of smoked pork and cinnamon apples overloaded her senses when she stepped onto the wide front porch and entered the farmhouse. The heavenly scents reminded her she hadn't had much lunch. The morning tour had stretched until after noon, and she'd had two phone meetings with potential clients afterward. On top of that, Holden's surprise appearance killed her appetite anyway.

"Kit, is that you?" her mother called from the kitchen. "Come test this."

She rounded the corner from the hallway into the large, bright kitchen, newly remodeled by Jordan and two orchard hands. Sonya Wendell and Rose hovered over a casserole dish cooling on the stovetop, two steaming spoons poised in mid-air.

"It's a new sweet potato casserole recipe," Kit's sister Janie offered. She held a stack of plates as she circled the oblong table in the open dining room, setting one down at each seat. "Mom's experimenting again." She punctuated her poorly suppressed grin with an eye roll.

"What's wrong with the old recipe?" She walked over to the stove where her mother handed her a spoon, too.

"Just wanted to make a few tweaks," Sonya said.

She wasted no time sampling; she was starving after all. But when her tongue caught fire instead of tasting the mild, familiar sweetness, she coughed. The surprise also quashed any constructive feedback that would normally come to mind.

"Do you like it?" Sonya asked.

"Or hate it?" Rose offered. She sampled her own spoon, closed her eyes, and pressed a hand against her chest. "So good."

Janie caught her eye and nodded. "She definitely hates it."

Sonya huffed in denial. "Give her time. She's still thinking."

"Well?" her sisters and mother prompted in unison.

She smacked her lips together, shaking her head. Her grandmother's traditional recipe was way better.

"I'm sorry but I can't even pretend." The bitter taste lingered. "What did you put in there?"

Sonya frowned. "It's a savory version. Garlic, cayenne." She gave a dismissive wave after tasting her own spoon. "Never mind. I'll toss the recipe."

That drew shouts of indignation from Rose and Janie.

"*We* like it," Janie said. "Kit isn't known for her discerning palate, you know."

Rose threw an arm around Janie in solidarity. "Right?"

Kit sat down at the table while her sisters and mother continued the debate about whether the recipe was a keeper or not.

"What's the commotion?"

Aaron Wendell, patriarch and third-generation owner and general contractor of Wendell Homes, lumbered in the back door, looking just as beat as Kit felt. He washed his hands as his wife and two daughters talked over one another about altering the recipe—a topic Kit was happy to avoid—then settled at the table opposite Kit.

"What's new at Love's Landing?" he asked, pouring himself a glass of sweet tea from the pitcher in front of him.

Kit leaned back, stretching her legs. "Not much. I had a lively bunch this morning. A hiking club from Bedden."

"On the boat?" Her father chuckled. "So much for hiking."

"That's what I thought, but who am I to question when they're paying me?"

"True. And you're still filling up the calendar?"

She nodded while he poured her some tea, too. "I have just a few dates still open this month, and more than half are already filled for November."

"And you're prepared for business to drop off during winter?"

"I am. I'll be officially closed for tours after Thanksgiving weekend."

She and her father had spent last winter applying fresh sealant and paint inside the boat garage she'd rented downstream in Greenhaven. The new and improved *Dolly Swain* made its maiden voyage a few miles up the river in March to Love's Landing. There were still small projects to tend to like the perpetually loose ladder rung and replacing ripped vinyl cushions on the seventeen-seat boat, but she rode smoothly. Tours had been solidly booked this year since her first paid excursion of the season in the last half of April.

"Have I told you how proud I am of you lately?" her father asked.

She smiled. "You have. I think it was yesterday."

"I don't know why it surprises me that you got that old battered boat up and running in time for the season. You give a hundred and ten percent to everything you touch." He held up his tea glass for a toast. "From driving semis to restoring boats, you're a dynamo."

She clinked her plastic cup against his. "Thanks. You probably never thought I'd settle back in town, did you?"

"Nope. Of the four of you, I figured you'd be long gone after high school."

She'd stayed away for years. After community college, Kit had made her way from coast to coast many times, first as a truck driver right out of community college, then as a team transport member of a dog rescue group in eastern Nebraska. Growing up, she'd apprenticed for her father's business as he taught her the basics of carpentry. That allowed her to pick up odd jobs as she skipped around the country, settling for a year or two in different places, trying them on for size. Eventually, Kit had grown tired of leading the nomad life, feeling untethered rather than free. She landed back in Port Chance just before her thirtieth birthday and had stayed put ever since.

"You can take the girl out of the small town, but you can't take the small town out of the girl." She peeled off her sweater in the hot kitchen, draping it over the chair. "It's like a magnet."

"Speaking of moving away, someone told me Holden Berne is back in town," her father said.

In her peripheral vision, a face or two turned her way, and Janie might have let out a little gasp.

"Yes, he is." Her hands clenched underneath the table. She did not want to linger on the topic of Holden showing up in Port Chance. Every nuance of their encounter today felt visible on her face as it was. It was bad enough he'd popped in and out of her thoughts all day.

"So you saw him?" her father asked. His attention stayed on his finger as he traced the rim of his cup, but Kit noticed a hint of a smile.

Nooo, don't ask me that!

"Sort of." She couldn't lie.

Janie pulled out a chair in a flash, resting her chin in her palm.

"Spill it," she said.

"He didn't come to see me." She rested her folded hands on the table, concentrating on cleaning a spot of dirt from underneath her nail.

"Right," Janie said. "He always had a thing for you."

"You're so wrong about that." Her face flushed. It must be the oven heating the room.

Across the room, Rose snorted. Kit shot her sister a look.

"It'd be nice to catch up with him. What's he doing these days?" their mother asked.

"No idea."

Aside from her sisters' teasing, Kit's family had never suspected there might be something between her and Holden. To the Wendells, he'd simply been her best friend. She'd struggled to keep her true feelings a secret then, and there certainly wasn't any reason to clear the air now, almost twenty years later.

"Is he staying in town for a while?" Janie asked.

"He didn't say."

"Aren't you a fountain of information," Janie teased. She sat back in her chair, squinting like she might see inside Kit's head if she concentrated hard enough. Janie, like her, didn't mince words. She was outspoken, funny, and a bundle of energy, also like her. They took after their father, whereas Rose and Sadie were more like Sonya. Calm and soft-spoken.

"I can't offer anything if there's nothing to tell." She shrugged.

Janie's shoulders dropped. Their father picked up his phone. On the other side of the kitchen, Rose took something else from the oven to hand to Sonya while she updated them about progress at the new storefront for Apple Hill Farm's bakery downtown. They knew that once she clammed up, Kit was sealed tighter than a boat's hatch in a storm.

The topic of Holden Berne was forgotten.

At least for now.

* * *

After dinner, they gathered around the fire pit in the backyard until Jordan and the boys headed to the barn to tend to the animals. Kit stayed long enough to replenish the wood box next to the pit, but her yawns prompted a sympathetic look from Sonya.

"You should head home and make it an early night."

Kit rubbed her face. She'd be out as soon as her head hit the pillow.

"I think I'll take you up on that. I wish I could stay longer."

Her mother reached over the arm of her lawn chair to take Kit's hand. "It's not like we never see you."

That was true. The little Cape Cod she'd painstakingly brought back to life after buying the ramshackle home was right down the road from her parents. It was an odd week if she didn't see one or both of them every other day, returning a borrowed tool or sharing a sample of Sonya's cooking.

Kit drove home with her window open, enjoying the cool fall air in an effort to stay awake, and her thoughts once again turned to Holden

She sighed.

Figures he'd show his face again at almost the exact place where they'd parted ways. *And why'd he have to look so good?*

Her hand tightened around the steering wheel as snippets of the last day she saw him that summer of their senior year flashed in her mind.

The lock he'd showed her with their initials etched onto its face.

Pure joy when she'd thought it meant Holden loved her.

But then he'd shattered her heart in the next moment.

We're best friends, Kit. We should have a lock on this fence, don't you think?

That's not what all these other locks mean, she'd told him. *I don't want it.*

She'd watched him walk away with an unreadable expression.

Within two weeks, he'd left for basic training. No parting phone call. No goodbye.

Kit shook her head as the bitter memory washed over her.

A few minutes later, she turned onto her street. The homes in her neighborhood were set on large, tree-shaded lots. When she pulled into her driveway, she rolled up her window and shut off the engine. Outside, the crickets chirped their autumn melody. The rustle of leaves overhead lifted the stray hairs from her face that had escaped from her braid.

She stopped on her way to the front door.

Lights shining through the windows of the house next door caught her attention, and her heart sank.

New renters?

She'd enjoyed the quiet since the last bunch had moved out. The loud music and engines revving at all hours got on her nerves, especially after a long day. This wasn't the first time she'd noticed lights this week. A time or two last week had caught her attention, but there was no sign of anyone during the day. Maybe the Wheelers were giving the place a deep cleaning or painting. If this meant she'd soon have new neighbors, Kit hoped they were easier to live next to than the last ones. Although, after her unpleasant encounter with Port Chance's latest arrival earlier that morning, any newcomer would be more welcome than Holden Berne.

Maybe tomorrow she'd bring over a bag of apples from the farm as a welcome gesture. As much as she relished not having neighbors, she might as well embrace the reality.

Chapter Four

"When was the last time you came back to town?" Holden's friend Dan asked the next day as they sat inside Daisy Gap Café in downtown Port Chance, finishing an early lunch. Holden hadn't expected him to visit until there was a solid date set for a shoreline tour, but his old friend told him he'd been on the lookout for an excuse to escape the office.

The diner's owner, Monte, called out orders as he slid steaming plates onto the window ledge between the kitchen and the dining room. The café buzzed with conversation. The place still sported the red vinyl booths and striking black-and-white checkerboard floor. The framed, autographed photos of the celebrities who had passed through town still decorated the walls. Neither the restaurant nor Monte himself had changed since he left town.

Holden sipped his coffee and winced.

Too hot.

He set the mug down on the saucer and scooped some ice from his water glass. On the other side of the table, Dan stuck his finger in the air to signal for the waitress while he waited for Holden's answer.

"I was here for a wedding this past spring." Holden stirred the coffee and sipped. *Better.* "Before that, I can't even remember. Ten years, maybe?"

Dan snorted. "And you never wanted to move back?"

"Nope. It's too small for my big-city dreams." He laughed. "I felt a tad claustrophobic like most eighteen-year-olds. Couldn't wait to escape."

"Have we really known each other that long?" asked Dan. "Almost twenty years?"

"Time flies."

Dan rubbed the ring of condensation his water glass left on the table. He was overdressed for the autumn day. His slightly unkempt beard and narrow face gave him the appearance of a wolf. But Dan was more teddy bear than anything else.

"How have you been doing since the funeral?" Dan asked.

Holden sighed. "Some days are rougher than others. You?"

Dan nodded. "Same."

Their good friend Jared, a guy from the same platoon, had passed away unexpectedly last month after contracting a rare bacterial infection. He'd left behind a wife and two young kids. Dan, Jared, and Holden had stayed close even after Jared returned to his home state of Georgia. The news had hit Holden hard when Dan broke it to him over the phone.

Holden shook his head. "Sometimes I get a momentary flash of him not being here anymore. It just doesn't seem real."

"I know what you mean." Dan gazed out the café window.

They ate in silence for the next few minutes, the weight of their friend's death settling between them. Dan finished off the last of his chips and pushed the plate to the edge of the table.

"So there's no one here who you keep in touch with?" Dan asked a few minutes later.

"The friends that I still talk to left years ago." He scraped the last bit of berry filling from his plate. Daisy Gap Café still had the best pie around. Kit was missing out if what she claimed was even the truth. "The town still looks the same, though."

"They're lucky here. When that levee broke, the flooding was confined to the lower spots at the bottom of the hill. It could have been a lot worse, with the exception of that restaurant that's being rebuilt," Dan said. "That surge must have been something to see."

Dan was right. The Yellow Pier Restaurant suffered the wrath of the springtime flood last year. Since Port Chance sat on the bluffs overlooking the Mississippi, Main Street followed the contours of the sloping landscape. The café and most of the other businesses lined upper Main Street. The Yellow Pier happened to rest on the lowest spot near the river. He'd heard the clean-up effort to shovel a foot of mud from inside the restaurant was cut short when the whole building, weakened by age and water, collapsed within weeks after the flood swept through town. Luckily, no one had been inside when it went down. He'd passed a construction crew framing the new restaurant on the way to the café this morning.

The waitress set their bill on the table when Dan told her they were ready to leave. He pulled out his wallet.

"Portia said the governor hadn't gotten back to you guys about the tour date yet," Dan said. "Do you think there's a chance?"

"I'm hoping. It's always nice to secure state support for a clean-up project. It's a high-profile tourist area." He set his fork across the plate and crumpled his napkin.

"Last time I looked at EcoPartners' annual report, you weren't hurting for funds."

"We're not. Sixty-five percent is funded by corporations. Another twenty or so by individuals. What government funding we do get isn't solicited by us. They're always on the look-out for the feel-good projects and photo ops." He shrugged. "The recognition would be nice, though."

Dan nodded. "Where are you going to get a boat?"

Funny how one word now initiated the scintillating memory of his interaction with Kit. Her surprised reaction, their dip in the river. That darned wet shirt. He'd left a girl behind in Port Chance and returned to a woman. *Surreal.*

"You're smiling."

His attention snapped back to Dan, and he rubbed his face. "Sorry. Just remembering a conversation about...boats."

Dan chuckled with a dubious look.

"There's someone in Port Chance. I have to find out if she's available first, but—"

"She?" Dan cocked a brow.

"An old friend. She runs a tour company in town."

"And she gives *boat* tours?"

He nodded. Maybe it was a little unusual that Muddy Bottom Tours was a woman-owned company. But then Kit *was* unusual. He'd never met anyone like her.

Dan shot him a sly look. "I'm beginning to put together the pieces. You've been slowly working your way north for a while now. But I wondered why you'd skipped fifty miles of river and set your sights here."

"It's nothing like that. The flood caught my attention. It's my hometown." He lifted a shoulder while tracing the rim of his mug with a finger. "I want to do my part."

Dan nodded. "If you say so."

"And you'll still join us if I can get that meeting?"

"Like I told Portia, if you manage to get a Des Moines faction here, I'll be back up here in a heartbeat," Dan said, tucking some bills underneath the cream pitcher for a tip. "The state has bypassed the Corps with funding for two years now. It'd be nice to bend someone's ear about that in person."

They left the booth and headed outside.

Down the street, the buzz of electric saws cut through the otherwise peaceful late morning. Holden breathed in the scent of freshly cut wood mingled with the fragrant fallen leaves. His gaze was drawn to the river peeking between the buildings on the opposite side of the street. Jumpin' John's antique store hid the area around Love's Landing. Was Kit's boat sitting at the dock, or had she taken it out for a tour?

As they walked back to Dan's car, Holden pointed out his old stomping grounds when he'd still called Port Chance home. Herrold's, of course, where the neon orange cream slushie sign still hung in the front window, blinking in all of its tangerine-and-turquoise glory. It was hard to miss Jumpin' John's place, and not just because of the squeaky metal sign swinging by rusty chains from the awning. His yard in front of the shop displayed a menagerie of antique farm equipment, vintage bicycles, and wagon wheels—*lots* of wagon wheels.

Dan's phone buzzed in his back pocket.

"This is my reminder about a conference call." He pressed a hand to his forehead, shutting the alarm off. "It completely slipped my mind."

"If you want to sit in your car for the meeting, I can take a walk."

Dan nodded before Holden even finished his offer. "It shouldn't take too long. Twenty minutes, tops."

While Dan climbed into the truck for the meeting, Holden continued his walk up Main Street.

Passing over the footbridge spanning the Huckleberry River, he paused to study the small tributary which he remembered never running dry. Now, its cobble-strewn riverbed was as parched as bone. These last few months had been dry all over the upper Midwest, a sharp contrast to last year's floods.

How many days had he spent down there on the bank, hopping from boulder to boulder, fishing, and building forts from fallen tree limbs? It'd felt like another world down there, cocooned within the ravine. Kit had usually been right alongside him and his buddies. She'd take it upon herself to act as foreman of any building project. He and the other guys were the laborers, muscling branches into place while she barked orders.

Holden crossed Main, returning a wave to someone passing by in a car. He continued on past the church and Hollowed Grove Inn toward Larkspur State Park where the trees blazed with early color. The walking path meandered next to a small park and a picnic pavilion, and the reconstructed cabin of A.J. Love, one of Port Chance's founding fathers. Eventually, the path led toward the Mississippi, where it split going either direction alongside the river. Stopping at the junction, he looked left toward Love's Landing. The sidewalk's curve and abundance of trees hid Kit's dock. He could retrace his steps, and avoid running into Kit if she was there. Or he could continue on the loop which would take him back toward the downtown. It was shorter. Dan might be waiting for him.

I'll chance it. Kit doesn't scare me.

And he really wanted another shot at getting that coffee and pie date.

But as he neared the dock and noticed the gate to Kit's pier padlocked, his hope of seeing her sank like a weighted balloon.

He ran his hand along the top rail of the chain-link fence as he slowed to examine another familiar sight: the dozens of padlocks hanging from the fence. He'd somehow missed them the other day when he met with Kit, so focused he was on seeing her again.

What was that saying, that change is inevitable, it's the only guarantee in life?

He smiled down at the locks. It appeared the tradition of "getting locked" at Love's Landing was alive and well. It'd been a thing for as long as he could remember, even though the flood had washed away a large portion of the fence along with many of the locks.

He squatted to study some of them, etched with initials, names, and sometimes a sweet sentiment.

L.H. + G.W. 4/13/2017
Angi & Harris
Marry Me, Bea ~ August 8, 1978

The locks were as unique as the inscriptions. Some were nondescript, standard brands with smooth or serrated silver finishes. Others were shades of blues, reds, and iridescent purples.

Nan M. & Reagan W. 2001
Preston Loves Eve 9-9-52

There were locks that appeared to have been made for exactly this purpose, to attach to a link on the fence. Heart-shaped. Embossed details. Locks to leave here, commemorating a special day, the hope of a shared future, two becoming one. And the keys, tossed into the water to seal the promises, now resting somewhere on the river bottom.

"Did you ever get "locked" on Love's Landing?"

It was Dan, already finished with his meeting, walking up to stand alongside him.

Holden stood. "Nah. Never understood the purpose."

Right.

"C'mon. It wasn't the place to go when you were young and in love?" A note of sarcasm rolled off Dan's tongue as he took a step back to read the sign hanging from the fence.

"Maybe for some." He stuffed his hands in his pockets, hoping to move Dan along.

"But not for Holden Out for Love, right?" Dan laughed at his own joke.

"I wouldn't say that. It just wasn't on my radar back then."

Liar.

"And I'm not married by choice," he added. "Tried it once, and it didn't work in my favor, as you know." He didn't like how defensive he sounded.

He'd married a girl named Elise Barrett he'd met while stationed in North Carolina. They met at the bowling alley where she worked, passing shoes over the counter to bowlers and serving food when the kitchen got busy. They were young and spontaneous, and he'd just found out he'd be shipping out in three weeks. Their marriage lasted exactly two months and seventeen days after he returned home from Afghanistan eight months later. She'd told him she was never leaving her hometown, and he couldn't wait to head west again. Her parents helped her hasten the divorce, with her father being best friends with a local judge. They'd never spoken again after he left North Carolina.

"No one special in high school?" Dan asked.

Dan's probing questions kicked up his pulse. "Nope."

I'm on a roll. Two lies in a matter of seconds.

His friend nodded, looking down the length of the fifty-foot fence until it stopped at a metal post. There, another gate led onto a dock for the next boat.

"It's charming," Dan said.

Holden huffed. "If you say so. Anyway, I'm ready if you are."

As they walked back to Dan's truck, Holden's thoughts lingered on Love's Landing, on Dan's question about there being a special someone. A familiar hollow space nudged its way open again, just the tiniest bit, but it was obvious enough because he rubbed the spot on his chest where he'd always felt it most acutely.

Chapter Five

Kit hiked her backpack onto her shoulder as she stumbled into her house near dinner time the next day. It'd been a long one, from the moment she rolled out of bed to find the wood floor underneath her bare feet unusually cold—nothing a fresh set of batteries in the thermostat couldn't fix, thank goodness—to the call from an environmental firm looking to book a boat tour in the near future for a project recon.

She didn't like those calls. A call like that sometimes meant someone wanted to mess with the river. While securing a booking was ideal for her fledgling business, she worried about the motives of these groups and their ability to shut her down, at least temporarily, for one project or another. In the beginning, she'd barely booked a handful of clients when she got hit with an injunction to stop the tours. A biologist and his graduate student needed to look at the proliferation of some supposedly delicate aquatic plant near the state park. The EPA got involved. Wakes and sound waves from the *Dolly Swain*'s motor, even a hundred yards away, could upset the ecosystem, the guy had said. She'd lost a week's worth of tours for that.

While she threw a load of laundry in the washer and popped some leftover pasta into the microwave, she sent a quick text to Rose, letting her know she was home and ready for Trav to spend the night when she wanted to bring him out.

Great! Rose texted back a few seconds later. *We're finishing dinner, then I'll head your way.*

Kit opened her patio door, letting the brisk fall breeze waft through the opening and into her house. She padded out onto her deck, collapsed into an Adirondack chair, and cracked open a can of sparkling water. The pop top let out a satisfying hiss before she took a drink. Her head resting against the back, she closed her eyes and let the sun's warmth caress her face.

Almost to the point of dozing off, Kit startled a while later.

Someone had shouted.

It didn't sound like Rose or Trav. She checked her phone. It'd only been ten minutes since she messaged Rose anyway.

Kit stood, peering around the foliage that cocooned her deck in a semi-private shroud. The large backyards on either side of her were empty, as well as the lawns which backed up to the far edge of her property line, separated by Little Horn Creek.

Huh.

Another shout, this time closer. She scanned the vacant property next door.

As she hunkered behind the privet hedge, hoping to spot the source without revealing herself, a dog shot out across the yard of the vacant house with something in its mouth. Seconds later, someone bounded from the deck in hot pursuit. They dashed around the lawn—the dog in high spirits, the chaser not so much. It appeared that whatever the dog carried in his mouth was a big no-no, judging by the frantic waving and darting of the guy having no luck whatsoever.

Wait.

She popped up for a better look.

It couldn't be.

But it was.

You've got to be kidding me.

She couldn't duck again in time before Holden, stopping to catch his breath, spotted her and gave a tentative wave. The dog, content to be momentarily forgotten, sprawled in the grass to cradle the mystery object between his two paws. That gave Holden the advantage, snatching it away before the dog realized his prize was gone.

Holden held up something limp like a victory flag.

"Dumb dog!" he shouted and shrugged.

"Not so dumb if it was within his reach!" she yelled back.

His smile flashed like a sunbeam. He pushed through the thick hedge that bordered their properties, then hopped her split-rail fence, scaling it like he'd been leaping over hurdles nonstop since high school. Her throat went dry.

Holden romped around next door like he lived there.

The reality hit her.

It can't be.

Maybe he was a guest of the new renters.

Please, please, please let that be the case.

"I had no idea you lived here," he said, out of breath as he bounded up her deck stairs, still holding the object which she now realized was a forlorn piece of meat.

Holden's flannel shirt, half tucked into his waistband with the top buttons tugging apart across his broad chest, gave him the appearance of a disheveled lumberjack. The breeze and the impromptu dash around the backyard had also done wonders for his thick, dark hair. It stood at attention, looking unkempt and artfully tossed at the same time. He was still as handsome as ever, maybe even more so now that the sharp edges of youth had filled out in maturity. She pushed all that aside because it wasn't as bothersome as the fact that here he was again, disrupting her carefully constructed, Holden-free life.

"Why would you?" she said, hating the higher-than-normal pitch of her voice. "I never—"

Behind her, the patio door slid open. Rose stepped out onto the deck, followed by her nephew, Trav.

"I thought you might be out here after I— *Holden Berne?!*" Rose hurried past her, throwing her arms around Holden's neck.

"No way. Rosie, I didn't expect to see you— *Wait a minute.*" Holden held her at arm's length after the hug, spotting Trav. "Tell me you don't have a teenager. Has it really been that long since I've seen you?"

Oh, he's good. He knew exactly how long he'd been gone.

"I can hardly believe it myself," Rose said, prompting Trav to come forward. "Travis turned thirteen in May."

"I see the family resemblance," Holden said. "Nice to meet you, Travis."

Rose shook her head slowly in disbelief. "So, what brings you to town again?"

Kit stood with her arms crossed during the whole exchange, silently fuming how easy it was for Holden to assimilate back into her life again. Rose acted like he'd just returned from vacation, as if almost twenty years hadn't passed at all.

"Work," he said, shooting her a hurried glance before his attention shifted back to Rose.

"Well, I hope you'll be sticking around for a while. It'd be nice to catch up. Our parents would love to see you again."

The snort that escaped her throat turned their heads. Rose pressed her lips together and gave an almost indistinguishable shake of her head as if to say *knock it off*.

"I'll be around for a bit," he said.

"Where are you staying?" Rose asked.

Holden tucked his hands in his pockets and looked directly at Rose. His attempt to avoid eye contact with her couldn't be more obvious. He pointed with an elbow to the house next door, confirming her fear.

Rose nodded. "Renting?"

"Yes, short-term."

She drew in the deepest breath possible, exhaling silently. Steam might or might not have escaped her ears and nostrils. It sure felt possible.

"What else?" Rose prodded. "Are you married? Have a family?"

Kit immediately noticed his hand. *No ring*. He caught her looking, too. His cheeks looked like someone had taken red paint to them.

Holden wrinkled his nose. "No. Divorced. No kids."

"We definitely have to catch up," Rose said, beaming.

Holden chuckled and held up the steak. "I'd offer to have you all join me for dinner but—"

Kit groaned. "I'll pass, thanks."

That earned her another scowl from Rose.

"That's so nice of you, but I need to get back to the farm. Harvest is in full swing, and it's all hands on deck," Rose said.

"Maybe we can have you out to the farm before you head home?"

"I'd love that," Holden said. He looked back at Kit with that self-satisfied smirk, like he was on the verge of cracking up, too. "Listen, sorry to interrupt. I've got this steak marinated in dog drool to grill. I hear it's a delicacy."

Travis, silent until now, chuckled. Everyone saw humor in this situation except her.

She and Rose silently watched him cut across Kit's yard and climb over the fence again.

"Why were you being so rude?" Rose asked in a hushed tone.

"He surprised me. I had no idea he's living next door." She ushered them back inside so she could focus without the distraction of her new neighbor.

"That's no excuse. You act like he's a sworn enemy."

Kit stopped at the kitchen table to inspect the pastry box of goodies Rose had brought for their breakfast. She clamped her lips shut to stifle the retort, which would prompt more questions.

"I'll never understand what happened with you two," Rose added. "You were such good friends."

That right there was the problem.

Chapter Six

Kit nudged Travis awake the next morning while it was still dark. Sunrise wouldn't happen for another half hour, but there was plenty to do before Mona Jarvis arrived at the dock with her eighty-year-old mother and seven of her friends.

They loaded Kit's truck with fresh pastries from Apple Hill Farm and a few more supplies Rose insisted were needed for this birthday party, like the box of photo booth props and one very unwieldy lounge chair since, as Rose put it, "an eighty-year-old deserves a throne and not some ordinary chair."

"I'm not going to be so demanding when I'm eighty," Travis grumbled as he hoisted the piece of furniture over the gunwale to Kit where she braced herself to pull the thing onboard. Her muscles hollered at her as she struggled to steady herself against the bulky weight.

Kit smiled as Trav blew air from his cheeks. Hanging out with Trav was a constant reminder of the simplicity of her youth. As much as she loved the life she'd built for herself, sometimes she longed for the time when her only concerns were rainy days that kept her inside and being able to sleep in long enough on Saturdays.

"When you're eighty, you can demand as much as you want." She maneuvered the chair across the deck so it sat front and center near the other seating.

"But I'm going to be nice about it," he countered.

She ruffled his hair. "I can't imagine you as anything but a sweetheart, Trav."

"Stop, Aunt Kit," he said with a shy smile.

They looped silver garland around the railings and attached a custom-made banner on the back wall of the wheelhouse—with Tilly's bespeckled, smiling face looming large—which Mona had brought a day earlier. They'd set up a table for the pastries and mocktails, and arranged the last of the plasticware when Kit spotted Mona and Tilly.

"Happy birthday, Tilly!" she said. "Looks like a beautiful morning to celebrate."

Tilly, spry for her age, hustled down the pier ahead of Mona and stepped on deck after Travis helped her gain her footing.

"Thank you, young man. And thank you, Kit. It sure is."

Gift bags swung from Mona's hands as she huffed short, labored breaths, trying to keep up with her mother. "I prayed all week for a perfect morning. Looks like someone was listening upstairs."

The other ladies arrived within the next twenty minutes. Before long, everyone had settled onto the cushioned benches. Tilly donned a purple feather boa and a sequined party hat, and kicked back in the luxury lounger her daughter had glammed up with a faux fur throw and pillow headrest.

Travis helped Kit turn the capstan, gathering the rope. She

wound it in place, then headed to the wheelhouse, touching the bronze plaque hanging beside the door, which explained the history of the *Dolly Swain*. The gesture had become a habit to mark the beginning of another venture on the river. She left the door open as she settled into her seat so she could keep an ear on the lively banter while she steered them toward Dubuque. Travis knew his first task was getting everyone a drink. He played his role as maître d' with uncharacteristic ease. She knew he ate up their compliments like candy, even without glancing his way.

"Such a polite young man."

"And so handsome, too."

"Looks like his papa."

Kit caught Travis's eye as he poured the strawberry-mango mimosa into Tilly's sister's plastic flute. She giggled under her breath as pink flooded his cheeks.

"Most boys your age would be running for the hills, surrounded by a bunch of old biddies," said June, a younger, primmer, and more soft-spoken version of Tilly.

Kit suppressed a smile at the look on Travis's face. The compliments were taking a toll on his complexion which now matched the hue of the rosy drinks he served.

"Speak for yourself, sister. I'm eighty years young," Tilly said.

Everyone raised their drinks to toast Tilly.

For a Saturday morning, the river was quiet. Sunlight filtered through the trees to cast shimmering ribbons across the water as she backed the boat away from the pier. She waved to Thomas Hicklebourne and his young daughter who fished off the bank as soon as she rounded the point near the state park.

"Aunt Kit, one of Tilly's friends is asking for the drink recipe," Travis said. "What do I tell her?"

"Find out who it is and tell her I'll text it to her before she leaves the boat. I have it on my phone."

"They're also asking about the guy that came to your house yesterday."

She bristled. "Oh, yeah? What about him?"

"Someone saw Holden in town, and—"

No sooner had Holden's name left Travis's lips than four women converged behind Kit, jostling for position to look her straight in the eye. The birthday girl was front and center.

"I thought I heard Holden Berne was back in town; your nephew just confirmed it." Tilly planted a hand on her hip, all business, but it was hard to take her seriously while she was wearing the boa and hat. "Did he come back to see you?"

Kit kept her eye on the river, draping her wrist casually over the helm. "Now, why would he do that?"

"Oh, you're just being coy," another of Tilly's friends piped in. "It was a well-known fact you two were sweet on each other back in the day." Gert was outspoken and a little brash, but she'd give the hat off her head to anyone. Under normal circumstances, Kit liked her.

"We were *friends,* and only friends. If something's changed, I didn't get the memo." She glanced behind her as Travis slunk out of the wheelhouse, poor kid. He had no idea what he'd unleashed a minute ago by throwing Holden's name out to these gossip vultures.

"But that's not what his grandmother said," June said.

"How would you know what she said?" Tilly asked. "You and Joelle were never on the best of terms. Holden and this one were as thick as thieves."

June ignored her sister. "I heard he came back to see if the spark is still there."

"*I* heard he moved in right next door to her," Gert said, speaking to the group as if Kit wasn't three feet away.

That part was accurate, so the grapevine wasn't made up entirely of speculation and half-truths.

"So what are we missing?" Tilly asked her.

She could feel four sets of eyes boring into the side of her face.

"You seem to have it all figured out, so I don't have anything else to offer." She shrugged, keeping her attention on what was in front of her.

Mona stepped into the fray, clucking her tongue.

"What's everyone huddled around Kit for? Let her drive this boat in peace," she said, hustling them away. "The party's out there."

The women shuffled away from Kit while objecting to Mona ruining the fun. She took a cleansing breath and shifted in her seat. Mona hung back.

"They're a little much, even without alcohol in their drinks. Sorry," Mona said when the last of them left the wheelhouse.

"No worries. It wasn't exactly a surprise. Travis gave me a heads up."

"That's a good first mate."

Despite their interrogation, she couldn't help but find the humor in it. She'd experienced more than enough of her grandmother's card parties as a kid. The amount of gossip that had swirled around Mimi Wendell's kitchen would curl the feathers on a duck. She'd learned early on that the less she shared about her life, the less fodder there was to spin into rumors. People made stuff up anyway; there was no stopping that.

But the more people needled her about Holden's sudden appearance in Port Chance, the more she wondered what they knew and she didn't.

Chapter Seven

Now that Kit had discovered he lived next door, Holden hoped he might chisel a little hole through the wall she'd built around herself. He also hoped that the statute of limitations on his former best-friend status hadn't expired, that it might count for something even if they hadn't been in touch over the years. Truth was, he'd missed her. And seeing her again had reminded him exactly how much.

So the morning after he invited himself onto her deck, he went to work, sculpting the long, lush privet hedge separating their two yards with pruners and the hedge trimmers he found in the shed on the back of his rental property. The backyard was a jungle. Aside from the overgrown hedge, weeds filled the planters. Several seasons' worth of storms had scattered tree limbs underneath the maple trees and an ancient white oak. The owners of the house, long-time friends of his parents, offered reduced rent if he helped bring the property back to life. By nightfall, he'd cut and stacked the fallen limbs into a half cord of firewood and cut a narrow opening where the hedge met the rear of his garage.

The next morning, a metal garden trellis blocked the newly cut opening in the hedge.

Huh.

He stared at it while he clutched his coffee mug, the steam warming the underside of his chin. Behind him, Sarge romped around the yard, snuffling every stick and mound of grass.

So, Kit was still being Kit.

"I don't remember being asked if I wanted my hedge cut."

He jumped. Coffee sloshed over the mug's rim, splashing onto his work boot.

"If I wanted to trim it, I would have done it myself," Kit added, now standing in full view on the other side of the trellis.

Kit appeared to have just rolled out of bed. If the wrinkled Hawkeyes sweatshirt topping a black pair of leggings didn't give it away, her hair did. The long braid she'd worn the last two times was gone. Waves of chestnut hair fell in wild abandon over her shoulders. He gulped.

"It was overgrown. Plus, it's on the property line." That sounded reasonable, though how he managed to string a coherent sentence together while Kit looked like...like that— *wow!*—he hadn't a clue.

Kit pursed her lips. She wasn't buying it, but now was not the time to admit defeat.

"I thought I was doing you a favor."

That seemed to soften her. Kit's shoulders drooped.

"Okay," she said. "It *has* been on my list."

"See? I can be useful if you'll let me."

"Being neighbors doesn't mean you have an open invite to do my yard work, though," she added. She fixed him with an unwavering gaze as a tickle rippled across the back of his neck.

"From now on, I'll keep my trimmers to myself." Starting the morning off on the right foot was his priority. He didn't want to break the news about what he'd really come back to town for until he had full control of the conversation. One wrong step, and *BAM*! Kit might go nuclear.

Kit plucked the trellis out of the ground and leaned it against the garage. She stepped through the opening and into his yard, walking a full circle around him and scrutinizing him from head to foot like she was shopping for a car.

She stopped circling. "I'm still not sure what you're doing back in town anyway."

"Oh, you know...work."

"Right. So you've said. But what, exactly?" She squinted, waiting.

The less she knew at this point, the better. Her directness almost lulled him into revealing more, though. It didn't seem that long ago that sharing anything with her was a natural part of his day. Aside from his ex-wife, he bet he'd been as close to Kit as anyone.

"I own a...cleaning company."

Her eyes popped as a little smile curved her lips. This news seemed to work in his favor, too.

"I never would have guessed," she said, nodding like the idea took a little getting used to. "Holden Berne, Mr. Clean."

"Right."

She laughed, catching him off guard. He'd always loved her laugh. It was a cross between a trill and a guffaw—pure delight.

"A cleaning job wouldn't have made my top fifty list if you asked me to guess what you did for a living." Merriment flushed her complexion. *Dazzling*.

"I don't do the cleaning. I'm the boss." *Time to move on.* "So tell me about your boat."

That lit her up even more.

"Do you have an hour? I could talk about the *Dolly Swain* all morning," she said, with the enticing lilt still in her tone, but then checked herself. "Not that you'll get the full hour."

"I do have time, as a matter of fact. I just made coffee, too." He motioned toward his house. "We could sit on the patio."

He half expected a protest, but she gave him a little nod, then followed him away from the new opening in the hedge toward his brick patio at the back of the house. After pulling out one of the metal chairs for her at the table and kicking aside a pile of trimmed foliage that he'd yet to rake up, he dashed inside to get a mug and the coffee pot. While he rushed around the kitchen, he worried he'd return to find she'd changed her mind and left. But when he closed the patio door behind him, Kit was settled into a chair, scanning her surroundings. Sarge had noticed her and trotted over to investigate. He laid his shaggy head in her lap. She massaged his ears—his sweet spot— and he closed his eyes in pure doggy bliss.

"How's the house?" She nodded, a slight grimace wrinkling her nose.

He froze mid-pour. "Do you know something I don't?"

She laughed again, letting her head fall back. The sound was so infectious.

"No. Well, yes. The previous neighbors were awful. I'm surprised it's livable." She stopped petting Sarge who protested by nosing her hand.

"Aside from a few holes in the walls, it just needed cosmetic stuff. New paint, carpeting. It works for me."

"You're an improvement. I swear there was some nefarious

activities going on here. All hours of the night. Each time I looked through the curtains, a different car was in the drive."

"That doesn't sound ideal at all."

He set the mug in front of her, along with the sugar bowl and a carton of creamer.

"You remember," she said, sitting up to add the cream and sugar to her coffee.

"You were the one who got me drinking the stuff."

"True." She looked at him through her lashes. "Confession time. I still drink coffee. *A lot* of it."

"I figured you did. No one is capable of breaking a habit like yours."

Kit's spoon ringing against her mug as she stirred was the only sound in the quiet morning. The shaded patio was chilly. Once the sun topped the trees and warmed the bricks, it was a cozy spot. Kit pulled her legs against her chest, cradling her coffee close to her. Sarge had given up on trying to regain Kit's attention. He was sprawled in the grass, lying on his side.

"Do you need a throw?"

She shook her head. "I'm good."

Overhead, a red-tailed hawk dipped in wide arcs, trying to avoid the handful of crows scolding him for his carefree intrusion in their airspace. The bird had caught Kit's attention, too.

"I wasn't sure at first," he said after the pause.

Kit lost interest in the birds and looked at him. "Sure of what?"

"That me being here was an improvement, compared to the derelict neighbors."

She smiled. "You were a surprise is all. I thought you were long gone."

Now that he was back, the reality of his absence hit him

again with a sudden pang of guilt. His departure from Port Chance had been abrupt in the sense that he and Kit hadn't been on speaking terms during the summer before he left for basic training. Their friendship spanned most of their childhoods, but the summer after high school graduation had scrambled any goodwill between them.

"So, the boat." Not that he wanted to rush the visit, but he wasn't ready to address his absence just yet.

"I bought her last fall after the flood destroyed my first boat. This one was a bit of a mess, but didn't have any major structural issues. I did a lot of the work myself. With help, of course. I know a couple people who'd refurbished old tugs."

If there was one person who could tackle anything she set her mind to, it was Kit. "How'd you come up with the name?"

She kicked her feet up onto the table. "A riverboat named the *Dalliard* sank in the 1860s close to where the Missouri meets the Mississippi. It'd been carrying cargo for the frontier towns and hit a tree snag."

"What a catastrophe, especially in those times." He loved how retelling this story colored her cheeks. "But why name your boat after the *Dalliard* in the first place?"

"The area it sank was close to where I bought her," she said. "Near Alton, Illinois."

"We've done some work down there."

"One of 'America's Most Haunted Towns,' they say," she said, making air quotes. Kit had always loved history.

"Anyway, the *Dalliard* was named after the captain's wife," she continued. "Dalliard was her maiden name."

"Let me guess—her first name was Dolly."

She nodded. "The wreckage eventually changed the course

of the river. It was actually covered in silt when a farmer spotted a piece of its paddle wheel in his field."

"I bet that put an interesting spin on planting and harvest that year."

"Sure did. His field became this massive excavation site."

"I wouldn't have been happy if I were him." He hooked his hands behind his head. "So you named your boat to commemorate the *Dalliard*. How does 'Swain' fit in there?"

"'Swain' is another word for suitor," she said, looking away to brush off her leggings. "It's a way to honor...the captain and his wife."

"It's a good name."

"Thanks." She held his gaze for an extra beat. Her fleeting smile hinted that she didn't trust his compliment. She resumed her focus on inspecting her nails.

He'd noticed the other day that Kit didn't wear a ring, and it came to mind again. He couldn't quite figure a way to ask if she'd been married before now, so he'd casually dropped the question in conversation with Rose the other day when he'd paid a visit to the apple farm. She'd been working in the farm shop. It was a slow day, so they'd had more time to catch up. *No, Kit hasn't married*, she'd told him.

"So you're giving tours by day, and..."

"Annnd?" Kit would make him work for it.

There was that unwavering stare. He knew people who'd cowered from Kit's eye daggers, though it'd never phased him. It did the exact opposite actually.

"What do you do after the work is finished? Spoil your nephew—"

"Nephews. I have three."

He nodded. "Are you building things? Getting into fights? I know you're not still breaking school records, so what now?"

Kit set the mug on the table and drew her knees against her chest again. "Not much anymore."

"Oh, c'mon. We both know better than that. You were never one to sit still."

"Why are you suddenly so interested?" Kit said it with a smile, but annoyance simmered underneath.

"And why are you so feral?"

The words popped out before he had a chance to catch himself. It was something he would have said to her when they were teens, and she would have dished it right back. They would have laughed it off, too.

"*Feral?*" Kit set her feet on the ground and leaned forward. "Maybe because you're asking questions a friend would ask if we were catching up after years apart. We weren't really friends when you left town, remember? And you certainly haven't checked in since you've been gone."

"If you're still sore about something that happened almost two decades ago—"

"I'm not. It doesn't matter to me one bit." She stood. "But I also don't feel like sharing my personal life with you."

Ouch. That hurt.

He didn't expect much after his long absence, but hearing Kit utter the words stung. His expression must have relayed the painful impact because her expression changed for a split-second. She almost looked sympathetic.

"Kit, I'm sorry." He'd overstepped. Again. He needed to tell her why he had come to town, but it wouldn't help the situation.

"I've got a tour coming in"—she checked her phone—"in about a half hour."

"About that—"

"I need to get going," she said over her shoulder. "Thanks for the coffee."

His hopes sunk like an anchor into a muddy riverbed.

This day isn't going to get any better.

Chapter Eight

The motor idled while Kit gave the deck one last sweep. The first black SUV rolled into one of the parking spaces on the other side of the walking path. Soon, a second and a third appeared, as sleek and ostentatious as the first.

As she swept the dust through the railing and into the water, her thoughts swirled around her interaction with Holden just a short time ago. A deep breath cleared the familiar jitters when he occupied her mind.

Two days.

That's how long she'd known Holden lived right next door. Forty-eight hours of stewing and grumbling under her breath. He'd been safely out of her mind all these years, then seeing him at the wedding last spring brought the memories roaring back, if only for a few days. Now here he was again. This time in an open-ended agreement with the Wheelers to stay in their rental for who knew how long.

And she still wasn't clear on the why part.

Kit tucked the broom into the small closet in the wheelhouse, glancing through the window toward the parking area again. Her tour guests still hadn't left their vehicles. The clock on her instrument panel showed nine o'clock on the nose. Government types always took their time, but who was she to complain? They'd already paid the invoice.

The trouble with Holden's sudden appearance in her life was that it triggered a sense of regret. She didn't like unfinished business, and she'd never been one to burn a bridge, especially one built on friendship and trust. It seemed almost silly now, to hold onto a grudge from her youth, but she still felt the lingering effect of their last summer together, of the blurred lines of their relationship and Holden presenting that lock as a sign of friendship. She pressed a hand against her chest, almost feeling the tangible pain in her heart again. Everyone she knew who'd gotten "locked" was in it for love, not friendship. In a matter of seconds, her heart had soared then crashed, thanks to Holden.

Yet Holden was still as magnetic as when he'd been the most popular guy at Bedden High. Broad-shouldered and broodingly handsome, his nonchalant swagger had parted a path down the halls of the high school. His good looks, though, didn't affect his attitude. He was as humble and easy-going as Kit was the opposite. They were quite the odd pair. Kit had sometimes wondered if she was his "project." He never admitted it, but she was so unlike the girls he'd made a point of flirting with. She often wondered how their friendship had endured the awkward junior high years and the shifting relationships in high school.

Vehicle doors closed, snapping her back to reality. She glanced at the vehicles again as a dozen people now milled around in khaki pants and zippered fleeces. On second thought, she pulled a stack of fleshly laundered wool blankets from the seat chests and laid them on the vinyl benches. It could get chilly on the water, especially near the areas on the river which weren't forested.

She'd laid the last blanket down when she heard footsteps on the dock. It shouldn't have surprised her, seeing Holden rushing toward her. He'd done nothing but catch her off guard since he'd arrived back in Port Chance. The chill in the air had reddened his cheeks, complementing the light gray sweater he'd changed into after they parted ways earlier. She took a deep breath to steady the erratic rhythm in her chest.

He raised his hands as if to calm her. "Now don't go getting upset..."

Over his shoulder, the group was making its way to the dock, too.

"What are you doing here? I have a tour starting, like, right now."

"I'm *on* the tour," he said with a slight grimace. "I tried telling you this earlier."

"What...why?"

"I'm hoping to secure funding to clean this portion of the river. I've been working with the governor's office on this."

"Funding for what? Wait, did you say *clean* the river?"

He nodded and glanced nervously behind him. "They're coming. Can we talk about this later, please?"

Her body temperature skyrocketed. He was a cleaner, he'd said. A simple, trite answer. He'd known a more thorough explanation would lead to questions, which might have also led to canceling this farce of a tour once she got a better picture of what it entailed. He'd purposely not told her.

"You bet we will. I don't know what game you're playing, Holden, but—"

"Kit, please. I promise I'll clear everything up after the tour."

She glared at him in passing as she hopped off the boat to greet her guests.

The young woman with a glossy pixie cut leading the group stopped in front of Kit.

"Kit Wendell? So nice to meet you. I'm Sirayha Rath from the governor's office."

She imagined Holden's eyes boring into her back while Sirayha introduced the rest of the group. He probably prayed she wouldn't make a scene, which proved he no longer knew her at all. Promoting Muddy Bottom Tours took precedence at the moment. There'd be time for the showdown later when they were alone.

"Thank you for fitting us into your schedule on such short notice," Sirayha continued. "Actually, Holden's office made the arrangements, but we appreciate the opportunity, too. Good PR, you know," she said with a wink.

Holden had definitely held out on her.

While Holden, Sirayha, and the other men and women settled onto the benches, she plunked herself into the captain's chair, fuming. They pulled away from the dock a few minutes later, and Kit leaned against her seat, straining to hear the conversation. No luck. She couldn't hear a thing in the noisy wheelhouse.

They cruised along the northern bank toward Bedden, Kit steering the *Dolly Swain* away from the shallow areas. Last year's flood had carved large troughs on the river bottom and dropped haphazard debris piles in other places. It was treacherous if one didn't know the water, especially for a medium-sized vessel like hers. She'd seen a few pleasure boaters rip gaping holes in their hulls after not paying attention.

A half hour into the boat tour, her phone dinged on the console. A text from Janie:

> Janie: Heard you're on the river with the governor today.
>
> Kit: Actually, no governor, but plenty of people from her office. Holden, too.
>
> Janie: How are you holding up?
>
> Kit: You know me. Steady Freddy.
>
> Janie: Right. I keep waiting for the mushroom cloud on the western horizon. LOL
>
> Kit: So far, so good.
>
> Janie: How long will you be shut down?
>
> Kit: ???
>
> Janie: The tours. How many will you have to cancel?
>
> Kit: Not following.

Heat flushed her face. What did that mean?

"Kit? Sorry to bother you."

She spun around in her seat. It was Sirayah.

"Yes?"

"We're wondering if it's possible to head up the river now. I realize that's contrary to the itinerary, but we have to cut the trip short. Someone needs to get back to Des Moines ASAP."

Janie's message had scrambled her thoughts. She couldn't focus. *Cut the trip short?*

"Is that okay?" Sirayha prompted again.

"Of course."

They'd barely cleared the point east of downtown Bedden, and now they wanted to go back? She eased the throttle toward her while the engine vibrated, slowing the boat for their eventual turn.

She glanced at her phone again, at the three undulating dots that told her Janie was still working on a response. Patience gone, she tapped in another message.

Why would l have to cancel tours?

The dots still wavered.

Against her better judgment, she pressed the call button under Janie's name and tucked the phone against her shoulder and ear.

The call connected right away, but the background noise was deafening.

"Hold on," Janie said, and Kit listened to the chaotic blend of voices and music fade as Janie headed to a quieter place.

"What's going on there?"

Janie groaned. "I'm playing Good Samaritan at the bakery, helping Linn this morning. There's a school group, and Linn's help called in sick."

"Gotcha. Listen, I can't talk long, but I need to know what you mean by canceling the tours."

"Yeah, I heard it from one of the teachers just now. I'm shocked this is news to you if others are talking about it."

"But what does that mean?"

"Holden didn't tell you?"

"Tell me what?" Dread tied a knot in her stomach.

"That he's come to town to clean up the river. That's what his company does. He's kind of a big deal."

Behind her, Holden's voice cut through the sounds around her. He stood just outside the wheelhouse.

"Janie, I have to go. Can I call later?"

"I'll track you down if you don't." Coming from Janie, that wasn't just a figure of speech.

Kit set the phone down and tuned into Holden's voice as he addressed the group.

"My crew typically can work a mile a day, give or take some depending on the type and amount of refuse," he said.

Someone asked how the area up river looked compared to what they were seeing now.

"It's worse. The river north of Port Chance never gets as much attention as this southern stretch because there's more commerce here."

There was talk about working around the weather, and how much could be done now compared to in the spring.

She strained to hear more, but the distraction from Janie's revelation coupled with the rumbling engine scrambled her ability to focus. She'd confront Holden about this soon. Her heart hammered in her chest as a familiar weight pressed down on her shoulders. He'd hidden something from her. Why would he do that?

Looking at the river with a fresh perspective, Kit scrutinized the banks north of Port Chance as they headed east again. The river's edge was indeed worse than the areas they'd witnessed south of town. Trees snapped in half mingled with twisted sheet metal, tires, and lumber tossed like matchsticks. Nearly everyone she knew who owned property along the river lost their docks in last year's flood. While most had been replaced, the destroyed remnants remained. She'd rebuilt her own dock within a few weeks, and replaced her little skiff since her other one had gone missing. Now she imagined it somewhere along here, crushed into an indistinguishable shape and hidden underneath the dead vegetation and garbage.

Kit glanced through the window toward the sky. She'd checked the forecast before heading out that morning. A twenty percent chance of rain hadn't concerned her, but now it did. The roiling gray clouds on the Iowa side of the river told her rain was imminent.

She eased the *Dolly Swain* against the dock a short time later. The group members offered their thanks, pausing in front of her while she anchored the mooring lines to the cleat on the pier, then hurried toward their vehicles to beat the rain. Holden hopped off the boat last and walked toward the parking lot, deep in conversation with one of the men. Kit zeroed in on his back, waiting for him to return with an explanation of what this morning was all about, and how it would affect her.

How fitting it was when he got into one of the vehicles a minute later.

He'd left again without even a backward glance in her direction.

History tended to repeat itself, and Holden was living proof.

Chapter Nine

All it took was an online search for *Holden Berne, river cleanup*, and her query exploded with a zillion hits on him and his company, EcoPartners. How could she have been so blind?

She shucked her damp jacket, draping it over the chair next to her at the table inside Daily Grind Coffee. Soothing strains of a mandolin playing as background music in the café and the hum of hushed conversation was just what she needed. The clouds had finally opened as she left Love's Landing after the tour. Steady rain tapping against the fogged window matched her mood—dreary.

While she sipped her latte, she studied her phone, scrolling through the photos and news articles about Holden and EcoPartners. He'd won awards, big ones, earning national renown. His company hadn't just focused on the Mississippi, but other smaller waterways to the east as well. His team led workshops, organized national conferences, and had a YouTube channel with more than three million followers. He'd worked as an adjunct professor for a few years at a private Missouri college, and had produced a series of TED Talks about being good stewards of the earth. The man was a walking, talking environmental powerhouse. It surprised her. Holden hadn't been as driven when he was younger.

But she also didn't live online. How would she have known this about him. Her sisters scolded her for not having a social media presence. Aside from her business website, which Rose helped with, Kit avoided computers as much as possible. She liked to leave Holden in the past where he belonged.

A *whoosh* of cold, damp air filled the café when the door opened. Janie, her hair limp with moisture, spotted Kit and gave her a scathing look.

"What are you hiding out here for?" she said as soon as she plopped down on the seat opposite Kit. She shed her wet coat. "How come you didn't call me back?"

"I'm not hiding. Doesn't a girl deserve a warm drink and a little peace when she wants it?" Leave it to Janie to find her. Her sister's snooping was far from covert. She'd somehow coerced the entire family into permitting her to track them by phone. Kit kept promising herself to put an end to Janie's hound dog ways, blocking the phone app that her sister used indiscriminately.

Janie tucked her hair behind her ears and planted her elbows on the table.

"So, what happened?"

She studied Janie over her mug, formulating an answer that wouldn't earn her an earful of unwanted advice. The sour taste of disappointment still sat on her tongue after watching Holden leave her behind at Love's Landing.

Janie caught on. "Fine. You don't want to talk about it?"

"Don't get all passive-aggressive on me. You have no intention of giving up that easy."

"You're right," Janie said. "I'll just sit here until you can't keep it bottled up anymore."

"I have no problem not telling you."

Janie splayed her arms across the table. "C'mon, Kit. I called you with that tip as soon as I could. Was it true?" Janie's fierce blue eyes matched her own, but Janie's were framed by a pair of sculpted brows.

She didn't have the fortitude to fight off Janie's persistent questions, not today.

"From what I heard of their conversations, yes. But Holden ran off before I could corner him."

Janie sat back in her chair. "I can't believe Holden wouldn't share that with you."

"I don't know why you're so willing to give him the benefit of the doubt. It's not the first time he's disappeared without a word."

Janie gave her a loaded look as Kit pulled up the search results from his name on her phone again and slid it across the table to Janie. Her sister spent a solid minute scrolling with her mouth agape before she spoke.

"I told you he's a big deal," Janie said, returning the phone.

"I'd say. Not everyone can score a boat ride with the governor's office."

"And you have no idea what this means for you?" Janie asked.

"Like I said, he left before I could catch him." She shook her head. "That's why I'm having such a hard time with this. It's not even registering with him how this might affect me."

Janie shot her a skeptical look.

"You weren't okay with him being back in Port Chance even before you caught wind of his intentions. What's that all about, Kit?"

"Nothing."

That was off limits. Janie could try to pry that out of her until her hair turned gray, but she didn't want to share. It didn't matter. She'd buried her feelings for Holden long ago.

Janie gave her a dismissive wave. "Never mind."

Kit softened in part because Janie was only trying to help.

"Sorry. There's nothing to tell."

"Oh, listen," Janie said, straightening in her chair again. "Rose is having a pop-up shop in the new bakery sometime within the next two weeks. I'd like to surprise her with a little added publicity. Mark and I are working on a promo video she can use when she officially opens, so we'll be there. Sadie said she'd order custom Apple Hill Farm Bakery T-shirts for everyone."

"Just tell me what to do. I don't have the brain power to be creative at the moment." She glanced up to find Janie wearing a sympathetic look.

"I understand. Sorry. This was the wrong time to spring this on you." She reached for Kit's hand to give it a squeeze. "It'll work out. Let me know what you need."

She rested her forehead against her palms, looking down at the table.

"I've got a full schedule this next month as long as the weather doesn't turn. What if I have to turn these people away? Some have been booked since I first opened." Kit didn't like the sound of her own voice. It sounded tired, defeated.

"You don't have the full story yet," Janie reassured her. "I'm sure it isn't as dire as you think it is."

Kit took her time finishing her latte long after Janie left the café. She dreaded going home to see the lights on next door. While Holden rubbed elbows with politicians and tended his illustrious career, she was left to fret about paying bills in the face of lost revenue.

Worse yet, sitting around in a stew of self-pity and resentment wasn't her way. Despite her grumblings and contrariness, she was basically a happy, glass-half-full kind of person. Looking at the bright side was much easier than carrying around a pessimistic attitude. Her moodiness lately had a direct correlation to a certain someone showing up in town.

She sat upright.

This shouldn't be happening.

Why am I letting Holden get to me like this?

She shrugged on her coat again, determined to de-Holden her mind from the questions she'd stewed over since he first appeared. No, she wouldn't wait a day longer. This needed to be settled *now*.

Getting answers from Holden would be her first step to reclaiming her sunnier outlook. Then ignoring him would fix everything else.

Chapter Ten

Holden rubbed his brows while studying his work calendar. It had filled up since he'd come to town like a pot in a downpour. There wasn't a span of even two days between now and Thanksgiving that was free of obligations. He usually left this task to Portia. Scheduling was part of her job at EcoPartners. But this was personal. It was still work, but Port Chance was home, and Kit's, too. Spearheading this river cleanup affected her in a big way, and he hoped to make it as easy as possible for her now that he understood the breadth of her business.

He hadn't talked to her after the tour like he promised. That bothered him. If she caught even snippets of the conversations on the river, she knew what was in store. Kit was sharp. And now he'd at the very least disappointed her again by not following up. But their interaction that morning before the tour left him feeling mentally exhausted. He could talk all day to a group of government types. Heck, he'd even spoken to the governor herself that morning by phone before the tour. But dealing with Kit was different. She'd always been his Achilles' heel. Her bluster drained him almost as much as her charismatic personality drew him like a magnet.

As he sat amongst the group on Kit's boat that morning, he kept asking himself the same question. *Why did I come back to Port Chance to jumpstart this cleanup?*

He'd convinced himself that his hometown needed him. But all along Kit was on his mind, too. Would she be proud of what he'd accomplished with EcoPartners? Might they rekindle the friendship they'd had in high school? It was probably wishful thinking, but he'd love nothing more than for their friendship to finally turn into something more.

They hadn't started off on solid ground. *More like quicksand.*

Portia appeared in the doorway.

"About those messages on your desk. That reporter called again. You may want to put that one first on your agenda." Her eyes bugged. "She's persistent."

"Got it. Thank you."

The flurry of messages to return had accumulated on his desk that morning while he'd toured the river. A note from the assistant at his Quincy office, asking if he was available to meet with the mayor from Hannibal, Missouri, about a volunteer clean-up weekend. Several messages from potential donors requesting meetings. On the top of the pile was the note from a *River City Times* reporter wondering if he had time this next week to chat for a potential article. He set that one apart from the rest and vowed to call her after he tackled the calendar issue.

He sat back in his swivel chair and spun around to gaze out of the second-story picture window. The postcard view of the river was what drew him to this rental when Portia had scouted properties for him. It sure beat the scenery from his Quincy space—the cramped and nondescript top floor in a repurposed machine warehouse. Whoever had renovated it scrimped on aesthetics and insulation. It was cold, gloomy, and in need of new flooring. It'd come at the right price, though, a necessity when he'd first started EcoPartners. But this building in downtown Greenhaven had him thinking he and his staff needed an upgrade. They deserved it.

The phone buzzed on the desk behind him. The caller ID noted it was his buddy, Dan.

"Hey, how'd the meeting go this morning?" Dan asked when the call connected.

"It went well. Just trying to figure out logistics. Not sure I can make this happen before the weather turns."

"Really?" Dan asked. "Is there an obstacle?"

"Kind of." He didn't want to share too much. Dan would run with it if he knew what stood in his way. Or more accurately, *who*.

"If it's permits keeping you from moving forward, I can reach out to my contacts in the field office there. Just let me know." Dan cleared his throat. "But that's not why I called. I want your opinion on something."

Holden stood and stepped closer to the window. "Whatcha got?"

"I'm thinking of putting in a transfer request."

"To where?"

He'd hate to see Dan leave the Quincy area. They'd stuck together since enlisting together. Their friendship grew throughout their time served in the Army, then working in the Quincy field office together. Once Holden started EcoPartners, their bond strengthened even more. Aside from the consulting gigs Holden pushed his way, Dan extended regular invites to his growing family's events—birthday parties, baptisms, and the occasional just-because cookout or game night. Holden felt especially grateful for Dan's friendship in the year following Holden's divorce. He'd really been there for him during life's highs and lows.

"The Quad Cities."

Oh.

"What's the draw?"

"We love it up there," Dan said. "It'd be closer to Sher's parents. Great cost of living. It's a pretty family-friendly area, too."

"I can't argue with any of those reasons." The traffic below on Water Street slowed to a crawl as the stoplight changed. He squinted, eyeing a particular truck that looked familiar.

"Meeting you up there last week just got me thinking about how much we've always liked the area."

"It's growing in a lot of ways."

"But here's the thing." Dan's tone shifted. "The word on the street is Jack's retiring within the next couple years, and I'd have a good shot at his spot."

"You don't sound as excited about that prospect as the first one you mentioned."

"I'm not. The money might be a bit better. It'd be a step up, and not a lateral move like the Quad City position. But when I saw the opening posted up there, well, it just felt right."

"You should go with your gut. What does Sher think?"

"She's all for it."

"Then there's your answer."

Holden liked Sher. Dan's wife was blunt, a no-nonsense type who'd traded her pediatric nursing job to stay at home with their toddler and newborn sons. Watching the trajectory of their marriage and their transition to becoming parents was amazing to witness, but he couldn't help the pricks of jealousy in his gut when Dan shared anecdotes about married life and parenthood. Would he ever have what Dan and Sher enjoyed?

Dan was quiet on the other end.

"There is a downside," Dan said finally.

"What's that?" He pressed his forehead against the window, trying to spot that truck, but the stoplight had turned green again.

Dan chuckled. "Leaving my best bud behind."

"Don't go getting soft on me." He sank into his chair again.

"You're right," Dan said with another laugh. "At least Sher wouldn't be able to get on my case anymore for our Saturday morning fishing meet-ups."

"There are plenty of catfish up here, too. Now that I have a local office, I'll be hanging out here more frequently. You can't get rid of me for good."

"Happy to hear it."

After Dan said goodbye, Holden tapped his pen on the desk, thinking. He'd be sorry to see his friend leave Quincy, but Dan's devotion to Sher and their extended family was admirable. That was the same reason he'd settled back in the Quincy area after he finished serving. His parents had moved down there to be near his grandparents once Holden graduated high school. He'd felt untethered though when he'd learned they were selling his childhood home in town. On the occasions when he'd traveled back to Port Chance and drove by his old house, a melancholy settled in his chest. His favorite tree in the side yard, a maple which blazed orange in the fall, had been cut down. The new owners had painted the front door red. A new gamble-roofed shed stood where his dad had built his old swing set. It was like looking at an alternate version of his past, vaguely familiar yet strange and out of place.

A commotion outside his office made him drop his pen. Seconds later, Portia appeared, blocking his door as she planted her hands firmly on either side of the frame. Over's Portia's shoulder, a set of sharp, blue eyes threw darts at him.

"I'm sorry, Boss." Portia set her mouth in a thin, grim line. Her chest rose and fell with impatience. "I tried to keep her in the foyer, but she's...not having it." Portia's eye roll meant his assistant's words didn't convey her true feelings.

He shot up from his chair, knocking his water bottle on its side.

It wasn't supposed to happen like this. He needed more time to sort out logistics before they talked. He wanted to put solutions on the table, to ease her concerns. It couldn't happen today, though. He needed more time.

"Kit, what are you doing here?"

Chapter Eleven

The woman blocking Holden's office door obviously had no idea whom she was dealing with.

A head taller, his office assistant tried dodging in front of Kit when she stalked into EcoPartners front office. The woman's size worked to her disadvantage, though, when Kit faked a lunge to the right then scooted past her on the left with ease. It was through sheer mass that Holden's assistant forced her way in front of Kit once again as they stood at the threshold of his office.

She cleared her throat. "I came to talk to you since you haven't given me the same courtesy."

It was irritating how her voice shook, not from nerves but because she hadn't planned on confronting anyone except Holden. This Portia woman still positioned her immense frame in the doorway like a medieval knight in a paisley skirt. She ducked to see Holden under Portia's tree limb of an arm, waiting for his excuse.

"What are you talking about?" Holden stammered.

"This doesn't surprise me that you have no idea," Kit mumbled as she stopped pushing on his assistant's beefy arm.

To his credit, Kit didn't detect an ounce of irritation in Holden's expression for her popping into his work place unannounced. In fact, he looked pretty accommodating. He repositioned a floral upholstered chair for her after he came around his desk.

Holden offered an apologetic smile. "Portia, thank you. I'll take care of this."

Portia's arm lifted like a tollway gate.

Kit glanced over her shoulder at Portia as she slipped through into Holden's hallowed office. Portia's stone-faced expression told Kit she'd probably overstepped by a mile, bursting into their workplace. She wasn't sorry. Sometimes it took a bulldozer to do the work of a shovel.

Holden waited until Portia closed the door behind her, then his gaze settled on her.

"Will you sit?" he asked softly.

"I'll stand, thanks." She tipped her chin to look up at him when he drew closer. If his eyes didn't smolder like warm coals, she'd probably be less polite.

"What's this about?" he asked softly.

Incredible. Is he playing, or does he really not have a clue?

"You left today without explaining what's happening."

"It was on my agenda." He reached behind him on the desk for a notepad. "See?"

His eyes widened when he glanced at her. What did she see in his expression—guilt? Good. She didn't want to be bothered with his list.

"Am I just an item to tick off? Holden, whatever you're planning near my dock, that affects *me*."

"I understand that."

"No, I don't think you do." She'd given herself a pep talk on the way up the stairs. *Don't lose your cool.* But her voice wavered when she protested. She'd always been too much of a hothead for her own good.

"Let's take a walk," he said, and his hand was around her bicep as he led her toward the door.

"I don't want to walk." His touch made little *zings* pulsate up her arm.

"I'm not taking no for an answer. I know you well enough to realize that if we stay here, it's just going to end in a shouting match with you stalking out. Let's go," he insisted as he urged her forward by switching hands. One was now planted on the small of her back and his other held her arm. The zings had turned into a small wildfire racing across her skin.

Maybe a walk would do her good, especially if that meant he'd hold onto her the whole way. *I can't believe you're selling yourself out because of a few tingles.*

They marched past Portia who positively glared at her from behind the desk.

"Going out for a little fresh air, Portia. Take messages, please."

"Sure thing," she said. Portia's eyebrows ticked up when Kit caught her eye.

They took the stairs instead of the elevator. Their footsteps in the stairwell matched the furious beat of her heart. She breathed deeply, willing it to slow down before she spoke again. It pulsed like a jackhammer.

A north wind assaulted them when Holden opened the door for her and they stepped outside. She zipped up her jacket and looked to Holden, who hadn't bothered to grab his coat before they left. With his hands in his jeans' pockets, he nodded up ahead on the sidewalk.

"There's a nice little coffee shop in the next block. Let's grab a cup, and we can sit inside to talk."

"The Coffee Loft?"

"You know it?"

"I do." She hoped Ginger had the day off. She imagined a never-ending interrogation if her friend spotted them together, her showing up with a handsome stranger.

A minute later they entered the warm confines of Ginger's café, which wasn't too busy at this time of day. Holden ordered them coffees while Kit chose a small table near the back corner, out of sight of the front counter.

"So." He settled into the chair a few minutes later as he set her drink in front of her. "Let's talk."

His complacent approach threw her. He didn't admonish her for bursting into his office, or for battling his assistant. Holden gazed at her and waited, almost like he deserved the scolding. She swallowed.

"You left today without telling me what's going to happen. I heard people talking about shutting down my tours, Holden. You don't think I have a right to be upset?"

"Of course I do." His dark eyes clouded with sympathy.

Again, this surprised her. She'd come to him expecting a showdown.

"Then you owe me an explanation."

"You're right. I do. But I didn't have answers for you then. I still don't. Yet."

"Why not?"

"These clean-up projects take so much planning. I started contacting the necessary people last year, a month after the flooding happened. There's a lot to figure out, permissions to acquire." He folded his hands across his middle, leaning back in the chair.

"You could have at least told me that."

"Honestly, after how upset you were with me before the tour, I didn't want to cause a scene in front of everyone."

She nodded. She really needed to work on reining in her temper.

"And here's an admission," he added. "I knew exactly what you wanted when you showed up. I just didn't want to involve Portia. I'm sorry."

"Fair enough."

She sank against the seat, looking around the café, but the only thing on her mind was Holden's power over her livelihood.

"So what I know now is that we might have to schedule the cleanup sometime within the next few weeks. It could be as soon as next week."

"Next *week*? Will I have to cancel my tours?"

"I'm hoping not, Kit. I really am." He stretched his fingers around his cup. "I want to try to position the barge in a place where you can still come and go."

She drew in a deep breath.

"Unfortunately, one of the areas with the biggest debris piles is right near the bluff at the state park," he continued. "And the river bottom in that area is shallow, even more so now after the flood waters transformed everything."

"It's a mess," she said, resigned.

Holden leaned forward, looking at her in earnest. "I'm well aware what this means for you. I'm going to try to not get in your way."

"You keep taking," she said to herself, but it came out louder than she wanted.

"What does that mean?" Holden planted his elbows on the table.

She fixed him with a level gaze. Now Holden was so close she could see the golden starbursts in his irises. She looked away again, disoriented.

"Nothing. Never mind."

"You can't accuse me of something without giving more of an explanation."

"Okay. Why now?" Kit asked.

"'Why now' what?" he appealed.

"After all this time away, why come back?"

"The flooding. Cleanup." His voice cracked, and he shook his head as if he'd given the wrong answer.

She crossed her arms, waiting.

He bobbed his head as he gazed at his hands.

When he spoke again, his voice had grown quieter, hoarser.

"Honestly, I also came to the realization that I might run out of time," he said.

"For what?"

"Listen, Kit. We used to be friends. You and I were... *tight*."

She laughed humorlessly. "And then we weren't."

"Right. Things could have been handled differently. I regret just...leaving."

Kit looked down at her lap so he wouldn't see the sudden quiver of her lips. She bit down until the feeling passed. She hated feeling so vulnerable, and it'd be worse if Holden realized it, too. Was this an apology?

"But we'd grown apart, and I didn't think it would have

mattered, you know, saying goodbye," he added. "That last day I saw you..."

Holden stared out the window for a few seconds, his brow creasing.

"The last day kind of sealed the deal for me," he finished.

She shot him a look and opened her mouth to say something, but then pressed her lips together again. What did he mean?

"I mean, you definitely didn't feel the same way as I did about us," he continued in a rush. Her silence had always made him nervous. "Anyway, what's done is done."

No, she didn't feel the same way as he did. He'd wanted to celebrate their friendship, and she had wanted *more*.

"But what made you come back now, after all these years?" Kit implored, not that his reasons would make a difference. She was just filling in the pauses while they finished their coffee. "You mentioned running out of time. To do what?"

"I'd hoped to reconnect. It's probably just wishful thinking, but I—"

"Reconnect?" Her heart skipped a beat.

He nodded, straight-faced.

Confused, she massaged the skin above her brows. A headache had started behind her eyeballs. "Where's this coming from?"

"I lost a good friend recently," he said. "We met in basic training. Kept in touch after our time was up and traveled together quite a bit. Now, instead of making memories with him, all that I'm left with are the old ones."

This was unexpected. Holden's pained look had pinched his expressive brows together when she looked up at him.

"I'm sorry about your friend."

"Thanks." He shrugged. "It's just that I don't want to come to a point in my life and realize I missed the chance to reconcile with you."

Reconcile. It sounded so *formal*, so void of feeling.

"I'm not going anywhere."

"That's good to hear," he said softly.

His hand moved on the table as he spoke, fingers extended, within an inch of hers. She imagined for a second that a zap of electricity might flash from her fingertips to his if the distance closed any more. Like it or not, Holden drew her in. It felt like nothing had changed now that he was here again. The same feelings pimpled her skin into gooseflesh when he was around, but the reality didn't please her at all.

"So...what I'm hearing is that you want to renew our friendship."

Holden's face clouded with uncertainty. "Yes?"

She couldn't hold back a laugh. Was he asking her permission? *Goodness. It's like junior high all over again.*

"Fine. We're friends. But if you expect me to bait your hooks like I used to, that's where I draw the line."

He laughed so loudly that he turned heads. This time he grabbed her hand before she could move it away. It was soft and warm, and completely engulfed her own. His hearty laugh coupled with his hand cupped over hers stirred a mad fluttering in her, like a cloud of butterflies had taken flight inside her chest. She eased her hand away and crossed her arms. Holden didn't seem to notice.

"I take care of my own hooks now," he said with an affectionate glint in his eyes.

"Good to know." Her pulse rocketed to all corners of her

body like a pinball machine. All for a little touch on her hand. *Not a good sign*.

"And to completely blow your mind, I even use a power drill these days."

"No," she said, breathy in feigned disbelief.

He nodded with a grin. "With finesse."

"And you can change out a bit for the right size?"

"Every time."

Holden had been the worst student in high school shop class. Lazy and more interested in yucking it up with his friends, Holden had given their otherwise easygoing teacher, Mr. Graham, fits writing referral slips to the principal's office. Meanwhile, Kit mastered the basics of building in that class, thanks to the foundation her dad had given her at home. Holden made it pretty easy for her to outshine him there.

"Mr. Graham would be proud of you," she teased. Tension still squeezed her shoulders, so she dropped them to relieve the pressure. *It's okay, Kit. You've got this*.

"I didn't care what he thought of me."

"That was obvious."

"There were more important things on my mind back then."

"Yeah, like baseball stats and weekend plans. Pizza." She ticked them off on her fingers. "What was that pizza place next to the market?"

"Pasconi's Pizza," he said after a pause. "It's closed?"

"About six years now. And we can't forget *girls.*" She pressed a hand against her stomach where a little pang tickled her insides. It had pained her to watch him flirt with every girl in his orbit. To make matters worse, Holden dialed his antics up a notch whenever she scolded him for leading them on.

"Girls were the furthest from my mind in high school," he said with an incredulous look.

She let out a good-humored huff. "False."

"What do you mean?" He looked genuinely stricken.

"You had a new female leading your entourage every week." She couldn't single out any particular name whom he'd have called his girlfriend back then, though. Why settle for the attention of one when so many worshipped him? But she did recall wishing he looked at her the way he looked at so many others. Like they were interesting, but she was something else.

"Entourage? Funny. They loved me for my brain," he joked.

He scanned the café while he squirmed in his seat. Even now, his comfort level dipped when she called attention to the obvious: everyone had loved him. Holden's unassuming personality was one of his best qualities. He acted cocky, but it was all for show. Maybe she'd been one of the privileged few who knew the real Holden.

Holden pulled a slow smile. "You ruled that school, too."

"Hardly. I was too ornery to be as well-liked as you."

It took him all of two seconds to nod in agreement.

"But *I* liked you," he said as his gaze bored into her. If it weren't for the good-humored spark in his eyes, she'd take him way too seriously, and that would leave her heart open and vulnerable again.

"Why?" she asked.

"I wasn't scared of you," he answered simply, then flashed a smile.

"Or you hid it well."

"When one witnesses the other getting caught on a tree branch by her training bra, nothing she could do or say beyond that point would be intimidating."

Her jaw dropped. "You remember that?"

"The vision is forever imprinted on my brain," he said between his chuckles.

His laughter was contagious. Her giggles turned to all-out laughter, and a coughing fit ensued.

"So embarrassing," she said finally, when their laughter died. She sipped her coffee and leaned back against her seat. "I can't believe we're having this conversation. Like it all mattered."

"High school is a transformative experience," he said. "You make all the mistakes and either learn from them or keep the cycle going throughout life."

It was strange, sitting across from him, listening to the same sarcastic brand of humor that she'd loved about him, but it emanated from the mouth of a man. A mixture of longing and defensiveness took hold of her again, and she tamped it down. She'd come full circle as an expert at denying her true feelings. *Thanks, Holden.*

The more time she spent with him, the easier it became to fall into the same trap again.

Chapter Twelve

A few days later, Kit spruced up a display near the front door of Rose's bakery while a slow but steady stream of customers trickled into the new storefront. With a momentary reprieve from customers, Rose let out a sigh.

"That was a whirlwind. I think I underestimated the amount of goods we'd need once again," Rose said.

Kit repositioned the display sign on the small table then turned to Rose.

"You'll get the hang of it. Did you ask Linn how much you needed before you scheduled today?"

Rose bit her lip. "No, I estimated," she said in a small voice.

"There you go. Linn knows best. You didn't make her the farm's bakery manager because her favorite color is pink."

"You're so right." Rose said, her forehead creasing. "But I can't leave the shop now."

"Call Linn and ask her to put together some boxes for me. I'll run out there and grab them."

Rose contemplated that by chewing her upper lip this time. "Yeah?"

"Yes. Why are you being so wishy-washy today?" Aside from Sadie and their mother, Rose was the steadiest, most level-headed person she knew.

"Am I?" Rose's forehead creased.

"Yes. What's up with you?"

"I guess I've been having doubts," Rose said as her shoulders drooped. She repositioned the pink gingham headband on her head.

"What do you mean?" Kit walked over to the pastry counter and leaned against it.

"Sometimes I wonder if I'm taking on too much," Rose said. "You know, with the boys still young. I don't want to take time away from them." She shook her head as she brushed some crumbs from the countertop into her palm.

Besides planning for this new bakery in downtown Port Chance, an extension of the Apple Hill Farm store bakery, Rose also oversaw the farm's gift shop and the event barn bookings. Her newest venture hadn't officially opened yet; it was Rose's third pop-up shop since August with two more planned in the next month before it opened in November. Jordan, her husband, had spent the weeks in between tending the apple harvest to put the almost-final touches on the old storefront. He'd refinished the wood floors, repainted the tin ceiling, and hung the newly framed vintage pie prints that Rose had found online. Kit especially loved the wall mural depicting a summer scene of a carnival on the riverfront, a nicely preserved feature they uncovered when they stripped off the old wallpaper.

"You're always with them, Rose. Driving them to school, taking them to practices, in the shop, in the kitchen, helping you set up for events. When are they *not* with you?"

"I'm talking about quality time. Anyone can drive kids

around." She popped open a new package of napkins and stuffed them into the dispenser.

"I don't think you need to worry. And now that harvest is over, Jordan can step in more." She rattled her keys inside her pocket. "This has been your dream for years. Enjoy it."

"Listen to you," said Rose. "I'm not used to you being the cheerleader of the family."

"Janie's taking the day off. I'm her backup." She wasn't sure how she felt about Rose telling her she wasn't that supportive. It sounded a little like her sister was telling her she was self-centered.

"What's Janie up to, by the way?" Rose asked.

"Helping Mom shop for the harvest party."

Rose stopped replenishing the napkins and winced.

"Confession," she said in a voice so low it was almost a whisper.

Kit didn't like the sound of that. "What now?"

"I may or may not have invited Holden to the party tomorrow night."

"*Rose*. You didn't."

"I'm afraid I did."

"And you're just telling me now?"

"I'm sorry. With all of this," she said, sweeping her arm at the shop, "it just slipped my mind."

"Well, you can just uninvite him." She turned her back so her sister didn't notice how her complexion probably matched her red sweatshirt.

"You know I can't do that. Besides, everyone will be there, so it's not like the focus will be on you two."

"What part of 'everyone will be there' aren't you connecting with the potential for someone embarrassing me? The chance for humiliation climbs exponentially with each Wendell in attendance."

Rose chuckled. "Oh, Kit. Please. You're being dramatic."

"It's true." Why was her family so bent on pushing her and Holden together?

"Do you think Aaron or Alex will make kissing noises behind your back or something?"

Kit huffed. "*Yes*. Six-year-olds are the worst."

"Not my boys." Rose picked up a stack of flattened pastry boxes and handed them over for her. "But I'll give them a warning."

Defeated, Kit folded a half dozen boxes faster than Rose could finish one. "I know they won't say anything. If I ever have kids, I'll need the blueprints for yours."

"*When*, not if, and I don't think it works that way."

She dropped her shoulders. "I was trying to be funny."

"Anyway, he stopped by here yesterday, and he was so complimentary. Jordan had just unloaded the tables and chairs for me, and everything was coming together so nicely, that he caught me in a weak moment."

"I'll just pray that something else comes up."

Tension crawled up her spine and settled on her shoulders. It was hard enough maintaining an air of friendliness with Holden without the *zings* and *tingles* of her attraction to the guy getting in the way. Adding her family to the mix sounded tortuous.

"Oh, he already said he wouldn't miss it. No plans," Rose chirped, flashing her a grin. "Said he can't wait."

As she hurried back to Love's Landing to retrieve her truck, Kit stewed.

So she'd be stuck with Holden for the night at her family's

harvest party. Intimate bonfire setting. Sharing s'mores. Laughter and reminiscing. So *romantic*. Too bad it was all wasted on her. Holden, too.

But then add the close proximity of the Wendell clan to that scenario, and it took on a comedic circus quality. They'd study her and Holden together, and she'd have to sit there like a specimen in a petri dish.

It sounded like a recipe for disaster, and she and Holden were the key ingredients.

Chapter Thirteen

Another fleece sweater floated onto the pile accumulating on Holden's bed. He bent over to get a better look at himself in the wavy glass mirror on the antique dresser. The small but useful piece of furniture had come with the rental, one of a few scattered throughout the house. So thankful to be rid of the last tenants, his landlords sold him on the fact that it was now partially furnished with all new updates.

A quick hand through his hair, and he'd be as good as ready for the Wendell bonfire once he chose a shirt.

He straightened and glanced at his watch, frowning.

Three hours to go.

Behind him, Sarge grumbled on the bed. When Holden caught his eye in the mirror, the dog perked up, cocking an ear.

"What are you complaining about? I should be the one griping since you're coating my sweaters in dog hair."

At the sound of his voice, Sarge bounded down from the bed. The clatter of Sarge's metal bowl told him the dog wanted dinner before Holden headed out for the night.

Holden followed Sarge into the kitchen and emptied kibble into his bowl. As he filled his water dish underneath the faucet, he paused at the sight outside his window.

Wielding a chainsaw, Kit balanced on a ladder next to one of the small trees near her deck. She appeared perfectly at ease even as the ladder slightly wobbled under her weight. A limb tumbled to the ground after she sliced through it like butter. A second branch fell.

He tensed as he watched her. A ladder and a chainsaw wasn't the smartest combination.

She stopped mid-cut and noticed him in the window. Kit's surprise morphed into a smile as she tipped her chin. Her hair, braided into a thick rope, hung over her shoulder. The midday sun glanced off the top of her head, coloring it a rich copper brown. While the day was a mild one, the chill and physical exertion lit her cheeks on fire. She looked strong and powerful. And so beautiful he had trouble drawing a full breath.

He waved.

Should I offer to help?

The last time he dared to do her yard work, he'd earned an earful.

That's a hard nope.

He'd keep his distance, lest he jeopardize their tenuous friendship.

Cop out, that's what it sounds like.

Holden stepped away from the window and leaned against the counter.

Here he'd been fretting over what to wear to her family's harvest party later that afternoon, and she's playing lumberjack outside his window as if getting together with him later on is the furthest thought in her mind.

Because it probably is, you idiot.

Sarge gazed up at him with his doleful eyes as if he empathized with Holden's predicament.

"Don't look at me as if I'm the pathetic one."

Sarge's tail thumped on the floor.

"Wait, I am?"

The dog whined.

"You're supposed to back me up. Be my confidante. Tell me I'm being reasonable when I'm clueless."

Instead, Sarge opened his mouth in a wide doggy smile, his tongue lolling out the side of his mouth.

"Thanks for your support."

Even his loyal, four-legged buddy could see through the lie.

Fine. He'd admit it: Kit still intimidated him.

Physically, mentally, emotionally, the whole bit. That woman had *owned* him since the first time she'd fixed him with her Clint Eastwood glare as a scrappy girl in pigtails.

Coming back to Port Chance and rediscovering the grown-up version of Kit—with the same fire, verve, and fresh-faced allure, only adult-sized—ignited that feeling with a fury.

He'd admitted more than he planned to the other day in the coffee shop. Their conversation started on a fiery note, but by the time they left the café together, all of the old memories and inside jokes peppered their easy banter.

And good gravy, why had he taken her hand? She'd reclaimed hers as soon as she could, hiding it in her lap.

But he'd seen flashes of something else when they'd been together. Lingering glances. A hitch in her smile.

Interest.

Or maybe it was just wishful thinking.

He turned to look out the window again, but Kit and the

ladder were gone. He liked to believe she was thinking about the night ahead, too. Hopefully, with a glimmer of anticipation and not dread.

Kit had never been satisfied with pat explanations. Her mind was always turning, trying to figure out how things worked. How *people* worked. That wasn't to say she liked all the touchy-feely emotional stuff. She just needed to understand thought processes.

His admission about why he came back was heartfelt, the truth. And Kit seemed genuinely sorry to hear that his friend's death had inspired Holden's homecoming. But he knew she looked for a deeper truth behind his words. This he knew by the way she tilted her head as he spoke, as if she somehow knew he held out on her.

Holden toed the checkered tile underneath his feet, letting his mind drift back to the early-summer day when he'd last spoken to Kit before he left for basic training.

The day had haunted him for so long that he'd learned to let the fragments of the memory pulse in and out of his brain like a silent film for only a few minutes at a time, then it'd disappear like a specter to hide until the next trigger presented itself.

Blue eyes squinting against a burnt-orange sunset.

The soft brush of her gauzy sleeveless shirt against his forearm as the breeze had picked up at Love's Landing.

Holding her hand for the first time *that way*, though her shocked expression spiked his uncertainty. She obviously hadn't felt the same way.

Then the metal lock she'd pushed against his chest when he'd offered it to her had been as sharp as her words.

I don't want it.

Chapter Fourteen

She rested her head against the Adirondack chair. Across the circle, Holden rearranged corded wood near the fire pit, looking for a piece to add to the flames. Travis talked his ear off about how his dad let him take the row boat out all by himself now. Firelight caressed Holden's features, and for a moment, Kit caught a glimpse of her young friend all those years ago when he threw his head back and laughed at one of Travis's corny jokes. The youthful expression, the lock of hair habitually falling over his forehead, the tumble of laughter in his chest. She smiled. It wasn't such a stretch imagining that boy and this man were one and the same.

"What are you smiling about?"

Sonya's brows arched when Kit looked over at her mother who sat in the chair next to hers.

"Just thinking about...the past, I guess."

Sonya's attention was drawn to Holden and her grandson again.

"He fits in here."

The words squeezed her heart and terrified her at the same time.

Holden did seem right at home amongst her family. He always had. Her dad had often joked that Holden was the son he never had, and Holden would then tease her about Aaron liking him more than his own daughter. He'd earned a punch on the arm every time for that.

"He won't be here long." The words almost caught in her throat. She coughed, and she wondered if smoke from the bonfire was getting to her.

Sonya leaned in like she hadn't heard her right, but her eyes loomed large.

"That doesn't mean he's gone for good," Sonya said. "But you have to give him a reason to come back."

She looked back at the fire, feeling a scowl settle on her face. Her attention darted to Holden across the way, but he was still engrossed in tending the fire.

"Don't get like that," Sonya whispered.

"Like what?"

"Your first reaction to anything involving your heart has always been to get mad. Why is that?"

"I don't want to talk about it."

"The silent treatment didn't work out in your favor the first time he left."

She jammed a finger against her lips. "He'll hear you."

Sonya settled back against the chair. "Maybe that's not a bad thing."

"Please, Mom. Don't make this a bigger deal than it is. He's in town for work."

Her mother nodded as if to appease her.

"If you believe that, you're not as bright as I think you are," she said with a smile.

Rose came over with plates of pumpkin pie piled with

dollops of cream. She handed one to Kit and Sonya, and caught Sonya's comment.

"I've known that for a while." She winked at Kit.

"Hush up. See if I come to your rescue next time."

"You'll never stop. It's your nature." Rose hooked her thumb toward Kit while talking to their mother. "Kit's Superwoman, didn't you know that, Mom?"

One of Sonya's brows hitched again. "Even superheroes need to be rescued sometimes."

Across the circle, Sadie, who'd been her usual quiet self all evening, said she had an announcement.

"I've officially partnered with another rehabber, one who has a bird rehab license. She also has a huge online following, which is something I'm terrible at."

"And this will help you with the money problems?" their father asked.

"Hopefully. The facility she worked from was sold. It was also where she lived," she said, tucking the throw around her. "So, since she's now looking for a place to live, I've been cleaning up the spare room in the house until I can get someone to fix the plumbing in the cabin."

On the other side of Kit, Janie nudged her calf with her foot just as Kit took her first bite of pie.

"You should help," Janie whispered.

"What? I don't have time for that. I can barely keep my own home running these days without adding another project." Janie, the least self-sufficient of the four of them, was an expert at volunteering Kit. "Besides, I already told her I'd fix some outlets when I get the chance."

"I can take a look."

Their chatter died at Holden's out-of-the-blue offer. All eyes drifted to her, then back to Holden.

"I mean, if it's nothing complicated like rerouting lines. I can replace piping and change out fixtures," he said with a shrug.

"That's a really nice offer, Holden. Thank you," Sadie said.

"Aren't you busy with the river cleanup?" Sonya asked.

""As long as the weather holds, and once all permits are finalized, they'll bring the barge upriver sometime within the next couple of weeks," Holden said. "Until then, I have some free time." He shot a quick glance at Kit before he tossed more of the kindling stacked near his feet on the fire.

"You have a *barge*?" Janie asked, her mouth making a little "o."

Kit shot her a hard squint. Janie already knew that after she'd shown her Holden's website.

Holden nodded. "It's where we collect and sort most of the stuff pulled out of the water. It's much cheaper than loading endless trucks."

"That sounds like noble work, son. We're proud of you," Aaron Wendell said, holding up a hand. "But please don't take that the wrong way. I don't mean to sound patronizing."

Holden smiled, catching her eye. "Not at all."

Rose delivered more pie to Holden and her father, then shooed her boys back to the house since it was past their bedtime on a school night. Janie also took the moment to excuse herself and Mark since he had an early morning meeting. As the circle grew smaller, Holden moved closer while her father rearranged the firewood, and Sadie and Sonya continued their conversation about Sadie's property.

The chair squeaked under Holden's weight when he settled in next to her. He looked down at her half-eaten dessert.

"You've fallen off the wagon," he said.

"Huh?"

"'I gave up pie years ago,'" he teased, throwing her own words back at her.

"I was being contrary. You made me mad that day."

"I figured."

She leaned over the arm of her chair, keeping her voice low. "That was nice of you, offering to help Sadie."

"Like I said, there's some down time," he said, matching her hushed tone. "And I know a thing or two about keeping a struggling non-profit afloat. Relying on free labor saved me in the beginning."

"I don't think animal rescue work has the same growth opportunities that you have."

Holden picked up one of the s'mores sticks and popped a marshmallow on the end.

"Who knows, maybe she'll become a YouTube star, taking her rescue work on the road," he joked.

"This is Sadie we're talking about. She'd just as soon let an injured raccoon fend for itself as be on camera."

"She's a Wendell. She'll do all right," he said.

That was one thing she'd loved about Holden, he'd always been her cheerleader. He was that way with everyone.

Even so, concern for Sadie was real, who was born to do the work she did, but it definitely wouldn't earn her a living. By day, Sadie did remote work for a utility company and the book-keeping for a few businesses in town. She'd always had a head for numbers, so thankfully that paid the bills. But she'd often said it bored her; it wasn't fulfilling like rehabbing the injured an sick animals that showed up on her doorstep.

"Starting out on your own takes more than willpower and a plan," she countered. "Luck plays a part, too."

He nodded.

"When I first started EcoPartners, I almost quit a hundred different times," Holden said. He waved the marshmallow over the fire, slowly twirling the stick. "Didn't think anyone would support the work. Thought we'd be laughed out of town."

"But you weren't because people believed in your mission."

He forced a smile. "Not at first. There was more laughing than pats on the back, believe me."

Kit picked up her own stick and threaded a marshmallow onto the tip. "Had I been around, I would have force-fed them your business model. Threatened them if they didn't make donations."

That brought forth a hearty laugh. "There's my former warrior-friend."

"Correction: *present* warrior-friend."

He bobbed his head, wearing a slight smile, while he watched his marshmallow turn golden.

After a while, she asked. "What kept you going?"

Holden didn't answer for a few moments. The pause after her question stretched until he cleared his throat and shifted in his seat.

"You did," he said.

Chapter Fifteen

K it glanced at him sharply, wondering if the smoke from the bonfire had plugged her ears.

"What?" A nervous laugh escaped before she could stop it. "How is that true?"

"It was you. I'd always loved your tenacity. You went after anything you wanted."

He leaned forward as she studied his profile. His soft grip covered her hand on the stick, and he eased it away from the fire. She'd let her marshmallow burn during that revelation. It was a bubbling spot of burnt sugar on one of the logs now.

"Only because people were always telling me no. I never liked that word much."

He shrugged as if to say, "There it is."

Kit let his words sink in. So she'd lived in his head long after he left Port Chance, inspiring him during one of the most impactful points in his life. While she'd beat herself up to keep his memory locked away where it could inflict the least amount of damage, Holden had lifted her up in his own mind. She'd become his guiding star. A positive force in his darkest moments. It humbled her...and made her feel terrible at the same time. Like she'd missed some important lesson along her own path.

"Anyway," he continued, "that's the sad, but thankfully short, story about EcoPartners' beginning."

"That must have been tough." She waved away the marshmallow Holden offered to replace on her stick.

"Hey, it makes for some great David-to-Goliath keynote speeches."

Kit deflated. "I hate to lay this on you now, but Goliath was the bad guy."

He snapped his fingers. "No wonder there are always so many people leaving the room when I make that reference."

Kit didn't like how the firelight danced in his eyes when he studied her smile a little longer than necessary. Dangerous, but captivating. That'd been the mantra ever since Holden had captured her interest *that way* in high school.

A few minutes later, Jordan raked the coals inside the pit, smothering what was left of the fire. A bucket of water finished it off with a short *hiss*. They all stood, gathering cups and blankets and half-eaten bags of marshmallows and graham crackers. Jordan bid everyone a good night, and the rest of them headed to their vehicles.

Kit felt Holden hanging back to let her parents and Sadie go on ahead. She rolled her shoulders as a tingle crawled up the nape of her neck. That'd happened a lot more lately than she cared to admit.

"Hey, Kit."

She'd anticipated him calling to her, but his hoarse whisper brought on a new round of shivers. The wool throw slipped from her shoulders when she turned, and Holden was there in an instant to drape it over her again.

"Thanks."

His silhouette was backlit by a gibbous moon, a celestial halo when she looked up at him. She drew a sharp intake of air, surprised to be so affected by the sight. Though the darkness muted his features, the outline of a smirk transformed his face. Teeth flashed with a smile.

"That was fun, huh?" he said as they continued toward their vehicles.

"It was. They sure love you." She squeezed her key fob and her car's lights blinked as it unlocked. She wanted to stay with him, shrouded in darkness together, but that was way too risky.

Holden lagged behind her, trailing like he hoped to delay their departure, too.

"Me being here doesn't cramp your style, does it?" he asked.

Kit opened her hatch when they came to her car. She tossed in the blanket. Sadie's taillights were already zipping up the long drive toward the highway. Her parents pulled away from their parking space next to her. Her mother's face loomed from the passenger side window, probably hoping for some...sign.

Humph.

"Why would it?" she asked.

"Oh, maybe because anytime I come around lately when any of your family is near you stop talking." Holden reached for the hatch and shut it for her. Then he braced himself against her car to face her.

"It's called being polite. They see me all the time, so I'm letting you visit." She really didn't like his intense, unblinking stare.

He was quiet for a few moments, choosing instead to look

down at his feet. When he spoke again, his tone was soft. "I'm just trying to get to the bottom of why you're so standoffish sometimes."

A retort sat on the tip of her tongue. For some reason, she clamped her lips together instead of letting the words fly. Tempering her words happened more and more lately. It was unsettling, but she'd been trying not to react without thinking through her words before they burst forth. Was it a weakness in the presence of his nostalgic stories and dimpled chin, or might this be a good thing?

"This is who I am, Holden," she said after trying to temper her answer. "I don't understand who you expected to find, coming back here after all these years."

She didn't have time to react before he took her hand, enfolding it within the warmth of his. His touch was different this time. More urgent, like he was afraid she'd escape if he didn't stop her. Stunned, her breath caught. His essence swirled around her like an eddy, and she'd drowned in it now that she was hooked. Holden slowly pulled her hand against his chest, drawing her near. She didn't resist, couldn't.

"Holden, I—"

He pressed a finger against her lips.

"Whatever happened between us, can't we just let it go? We were best friends, Kit."

She wanted to stay rooted in this spot for a long time. His nearness, so comforting, so *right*, smoothed over the sharp edges of her doubt. What if she did let go of her reservations? What would happen to her once he left again? The thought terrified her.

"And we're still friends," she said, willing her voice to behave. "We've already settled this, remember?

She bowed her head and closed her eyes as a wave of dizziness came over her for holding her breath. Warmth emanating from his unzipped coat and the flannel shirt he wore beckoned her. The smell of wood smoke and the piney citrus scent of his cologne was electrifying.

"It was so long ago," she added. "Do you really think I'd hold onto a teenage grudge all these years?"

He tilted her chin up with the finger that had touched her lips. His eyes were dark coals, catching the light from the lamp post by the barn. A soft huff escaped him.

"Yes," he said with a soft smile. "You're the Mistress of Grudges."

She took a step back, saving herself from imminent danger.

"What's wrong?" he asked. The skin on his throat rippled.

"It's late. I'm tired," she said lightly, then halfheartedly whacked him on the arm. She'd pass out if she didn't get away from him now. Her breath hitched when she inhaled. "And friends don't hold each other...like *that*."

He blinked. His mouth fell open slightly. "Like what? Enlighten me."

"Close." She pancaked her palms together in case he was totally daft and needed a visual.

"Oh, good gravy, Kit. It's just teasing. How old are you, thirty-seven going on...*seven*?"

There it was again, Holden poking fun at her. He was blissfully unaware of how he affected her. To Holden, hand holding and soft touches were signs of friendship. They meant so much more to her.

Holden waggled his head, getting in her face with that goofy smile that had always made her break down in a grin.

His words echoed in her mind.

It's just teasing.

It was hard to process what she felt for Holden without also remembering that day on Love's Landing twenty years ago.

We're best friends, Kit. We should have a lock on this fence, don't you think?

She opened her truck door, bracing herself against the seat as she faced him.

"My days of being teased are over, I guess."

Holden blinked as the corner of his mouth ticked down.

"I have a few hours to kill a few days from now," he said after a pause. "Maybe we can find out from Sadie what she needs taken care of at the sanctuary. We can head out there together?"

She nodded, not meeting his eyes. Her skin tightened with apprehension.

"I'll give her a call," he said as he walked around to the driver's side of his own truck. He hesitated again, looking at her over the hood.

"You know, sometimes it's like I never left here."

She acknowledged that with a tip of her chin.

"But other times this place feels like it's moved on without me."

"What are you saying?" She had an inkling of what he meant, but waited for him to clarify.

"I'm not sure," he said. "It's just an observation, me thinking aloud."

"It helps to stay put. Changes are more gradual that way." She'd felt that way too after coming back home. The sights and sounds of Port Chance had shifted since she'd been away. Or maybe she had.

When he didn't say anything, Kit cringed. She'd meant it as

a good-humored remark, but the undertones told a different story if Holden felt like reading into it. She hoped that wasn't the case as she second-guessed her own words. Kit wouldn't have even suggested he stick around Port Chance on account of her if their relationship had taken the turn she'd wished for. They'd both had ambitions. Holden had known for years he'd enlist as soon as they graduated. She'd head off to college.

"Very true," he said with a wince before climbing into his truck and driving away from Apple Hill Farm.

Chapter Sixteen

A late-night squall had swept through town the night before, depositing the last of the leaves from the trees near the landing onto the *Dolly Swain*'s deck. Kit spent the morning sweeping leaves pasted onto the deck by the fierce wind like they'd been attached with wood glue. An eleven o'clock tour was on her calendar today, so she'd finish cleaning then wander downtown to grab a coffee before her guests appeared.

After popping into Daily Grind, she stood on the corner curb with a little time to kill. Across the street, Daisy Gap Café bustled as usual. Rose's new pink-striped awning a few doors down was a cheery addition to Main Street. She was certain the neighbors on either side, Herrold's Soda and Sweet Emporium and the floral shop, were thrilled to see the long-closed storefront brought back to life.

Kit looked across the street to her left as the scent of fresh coffee filled her senses. She let the steam from her cup wash over her face as she squinted at the metallic signage hanging on the building on the opposite corner. She smiled at Jumpin' John

Goodman's little holiday touch hanging on the side of his antique store: a Christmas wreath with a red vinyl bow snapping jauntily in the breeze.

Jumpin's getting into the spirit early this year.

Since the weather had taken a turn for the worse, Jumpin's familiar perch on the old milk canister fashioned with the tractor seat stood empty under the awning as she wandered up the front walk. She pushed open the front door, setting the string of bells dancing above her head.

"Long time, no see, Miss Sunshine," Jumpin' crowed when he peered over the counter from where he sat. "How've you been this month of Sundays?"

"Can't complain. Keeping busy." She hooked her thumb over her shoulder. "I spotted your little decoration next to your sign and thought I'd find out what had happened to my Scrooge friend."

"Bah humbug," he answered with a toothy smile.

"That wreath is telling me otherwise."

"Oh, you know. My daughter got after me. Said I needed a little sprucing up outside. I wouldn't have bothered myself, but she came armed with a hammer and a ladder."

"A facelift never hurts business."

"Never mind that. It's not even Halloween yet," he said.

"The Christmas spirit lives year-round," she countered.

Jumpin' chuckled and slowly stood, straightening as best as his crooked body would allow. A tweed patchwork-panel cap cocked on his mostly bald head gave him an eccentric air, which to anyone who really knew Jumpin' wasn't necessary.

"What can I help you with today, Miss Kit?"

"I'm looking for a lock."

Jumpin' stuck an arthritic finger in the air. "Good thing I've got a healthy stockpile. C'mon."

Kit followed him down one of the narrow aisles, weaving around quilt racks draped with vintage linens, plus wicker planters and side chairs of every design imaginable. Jumpin' stopped in front of a primitive display case. Shelves covered in pink velvet showcased dozens of padlocks like they were precious jewels.

"Is there still a demand for them?" she asked. There was such a variety of shapes and sizes. Some looked new; others were pitted with rust and scratches. "We're running out of room on the fence. The city needs to put up more sections."

"People never stopped asking for them, even when the storm washed most of the fence away. Getting "locked" on Love's Landing put Port Chance on the map, you know," he said, straightening the fabric where it draped over one shelf.

Kit squatted to get a better view of the ones on the bottom. Some locks already bore initials as if they'd found a home on the fence before falling victim to the flood.

"See anything you like?"

"I'm just looking."

Jumpin' softly chuckled.

"I'll leave you to look to your heart's content, then."

Smart man, getting the hint she wanted to browse without him looking over her shoulder. Jumpin' was one of Port Chance's finest, but even he liked to bend an ear or two for a captive audience.

She slid the glass door aside on the bottom half of the case to pick up an iridescent green lock. Its long, oval shank was unique in that it was much larger than other locks. Someone had tried to etch a design on one side, but it was indistinguishable. The cold metal soothed the skin on her palm. She turned it over, finding the weight of it strangely comforting.

When she thought back to the day Holden had offered her the lock, all she could remember was the way her throat had closed up. He tried turning the ritual of getting locked on Love's Landing into something as trite as exchanging friendship bracelets. The memory taunted her. As if the most wonderful dream had been snatched away at midpoint and replaced with a nightmare.

Kit walked around the shop, holding onto the lock as she did, much like one would try on a pair of shoes to test the fit. She stewed about the contrast between painful memories and the reason why she'd been drawn to Jumpin's lock display despite those memories.

Stopping in front of an absurdly large collection of salt and pepper shakers, she studied the variety of shapes—dogs, Christmas trees, tiny cottages with thatched roofs—without really seeing them. Her reflection stared back at her in the glass door, unblinking. The lock grew heavier in her hand.

She wandered down the aisle and over to the next one, pausing to touch a neatly folded stack of embroidered aprons, and ran her thumb down the faded spines of a few books. When she circled back to the display case holding the locks, she slid the door open again and replaced the lock in its resting place.

Ever since the flood washed away more than half the fence, more people had come to Love's Landing as a kind of homage, studying the sign which the city had replaced almost immediately, adding locks, and taking pictures. Someone had started a social media page for Love's Landing so visitors could post their memories and photos.

"Did you find what you were looking for?" Jumpin' asked when she came toward him down the aisle again.

"I already have what I need after all."

Jumpin' nodded like he understood. "Sometimes it takes looking around to figure that out. Glad to be of help." He tipped his cap to her as she headed toward the front door.

She smiled, thankful she didn't have to offer more of an explanation, because she wasn't sure her answer would make sense.

Chapter Seventeen

Days passed without a word or sighting of Kit. On the night of the bonfire when he'd casually suggested that they go to Sadie's place together, she seemed lukewarm about the idea. It was clear that he'd upset her comfort level, judging by the amount of thread bits she'd picked off her wool throw that night. His attempt to pry open her willfully guarded self only ended with Kit shutting him down. He left the farm wondering what would have happened if he never left Port Chance. Would he and Kit have found their way to each other? Imagining that possibility cut him to the core.

Now, as he claimed a corner booth at Daisy Gap Café, his thoughts churned. Determined to finalize the last permit before the reporter showed up at the café, Holden checked his messages for the umpteenth time.

Nothing.

He needed to bring the barge through Port Chance and anchor it near the state park while the weather permitted. Time was running out. Someone at the Quad City division of the Army Corps had been playing phone tag with Portia since last week. He'd finally offered to take the task off Portia's hands, hoping to speed things along. His impatience for a concrete plan grew thinner as the days wore on, and he couldn't imagine what Kit was going through. If he didn't get approval for the last permit by the end of the day, he'd give Kit a call to check in. A little reassurance that he was pushing for answers would hopefully soothe her anxiety.

He tapped away on his laptop, keeping one eye on his silent phone and the other on the narrow view of the *Dolly Swain* docked at the landing. He spotted her truck as it headed past the restaurant and turned at the next block on its way to Love's Landing. He knew she was preparing for a tour by the way the fevered movements of her minuscule figure dashed across the deck, over the pier, to her truck, and back again. His pulse thudded in his neck each time he caught sight of her. Kit had wiggled back into his conscience for good, and he somehow had to figure out what to do about it now.

A draft from the opening door chilled his face. An auburn-haired woman wearing a shearling, knee-length coat walked into the café, scanning the tables until she caught his eye. He signaled her over and stood to introduce himself.

"Amy Warre. Thanks so much for meeting me," she said, and he caught a hint of a southern accent in her tone. "I'll admit, I had second thoughts coming out today. I heard we're maybe due for some snow later on."

Holden shrugged. "Possibly. That can change on a dime, though."

"I've not grown used to this weather yet, even though I've lived here close to two years."

"It can certainly be a bear if you're not used to Midwestern weather. I take it you've come from a warmer place?" He motioned for her to sit.

She settled into the seat across from him, momentarily caught off guard by his question. Then she smiled.

"Yes. Alabama." She pulled a notebook and a recorder from her bag. "You don't mind if I record this, do you?"

"Of course not." He braced himself as the door opened again and another wave of bitter cold bit his skin. "Though in all fairness to Midwestern winters, your summers are just as brutal."

"That is true. After a while you get acclimated, though," she said.

"How long have you worked for the *River City Times*?"

"About a year and a half. The newspaper I worked for back home downsized. My sister lives up here, and the *Times* is under the same corporate umbrella, so I thought why not?"

"Family is as good a reason as any to relocate."

They chatted about how similar her little hometown near Birmingham was compared to Port Chance while she readied her recorder. The café hadn't been busy when he came in, but suddenly a crowd of teenaged girls in Burlington High jackets and their parents crowded into the foyer. Monte left the kitchen to help his staff finish clearing tables in order to seat the groups whose chatter and laughter filled the restaurant. In the midst of the chaotic scene, an all-too-familiar face caught him by surprise. She stood against the counter, far behind most of the people, but the familiar pink boxes under one arm caught his attention.

Kit.

She'd snuck away from the landing without drawing his attention.

As she slowly glanced around the café, Holden froze. Her eyes flickered over him, not seeing him at first, until she did a double-take. Then, *oh man*, did she see him. Not just him, but Amy, too. She leveled a stare in their direction until Amy asked him another question.

"Sorry?" He wished he could trade seats with Amy so he wouldn't be in Kit's visual line of fire.

"I asked if you're ready to get started."

"Of course," he said. "Should we order first? An early lunch? Pie? Or can I just get you a coffee?"

The waitress came by at that moment, and he put in an order for a breakfast sandwich. Amy settled for a water. He leaned back in his chair and crossed his arms, tucking his hands under his armpits. Trying to avoid Kit was harder than he thought. Instead, he probably stared a little too hard at Amy while she peppered him with questions. If she noticed, she didn't let on.

"So given the nature of your work, and the geographic scope of the projects you take on, would you say you live a somewhat nomadic life?" Amy asked as she studied her notepad.

"Maybe in the beginning. Now, thankfully, we've grown so big that I have a whole team behind me, coordinating cleanups, running the workshops, etcetera. I step in when I'm not meeting with potential sponsors and other entities who allow us to keep doing the work we're doing." He paused as his attention automatically shifted to Kit, but she talked with Monte at the moment. "I travel between my Quincy office and the newly opened one here."

Amy nodded. "So, as the face of EcoPartners, you can work anywhere?"

"Basically, but traveling is a big part of the business."

"Where, besides in this area, have you identified flooding issues?" Amy asked.

He paused as he glanced at Kit again who leaned against the front counter now, waiting on the group ahead of her to leave.

"Flooding is happening all over, even in places that never experienced it before."

At the counter, Kit tossed him another side-eye. Monte brought forth two large bags of takeout, lunch for her tour group, no doubt. He wasn't fooled by the emotionless expression. He could almost see the questions churning behind Kit's cool façade. She left a minute later without another glance in their direction.

"You're from this area originally, so surely working here must have its appeal?" Amy asked.

"You bet it does. It's always good to come home. I'm thrilled to help my hometown in their time of need. They supported me while I grew up in Port Chance, after all."

"So this project in particular might be a little harder to wrap up when the time comes?"

"Yes and no. It'll be satisfying in the sense that my company was able to step in, make a difference. But saying goodbye is always hard."

"What in particular will you miss?"

He linked his fingers across his middle as Kit's face swam in his conscience. He blanked, couldn't think of three words to string together in answer to Amy's question.

Amy caught on to his long pause. "Maybe it won't be hard to leave after all?"

"There's Herrold's," he blurted, for lack of a better answer. "That will be hard to leave behind."

"Oh? What's Herrold's?"

"Only the best soda shop this side of the Mississippi. You haven't lived until you've tried their mint chocolate chip Snowslide."

"Good to know," Amy said with a one-sided smile. She signaled to the waitress who came by a minute later to top off her water.

Snowslides had been Kit's favorite. Her choice became his favorite, too. Sometimes when either one of them was short on money, they'd shared one, sitting next to each other, sipping from the same cup, their bare legs pressed against one another when they were old enough to drive there after school. The memory left his fork momentarily suspended in front of his face.

"Holden?"

He snapped back to the present. Amy's forehead creased.

"Sorry. Yes?"

"I asked about your next project after you wrap up this one."

Next one. The project. Kit.

His thoughts were scrambled like a plate of Monte's eggs.

"Or maybe you're not thinking that far ahead with winter coming. I'm sure your work changes drastically, depending on the season," she said as she looked over her notes.

He mumbled an affirmative and shifted in his seat, determined to push Kit out of his mind, at least until Amy's job was finished here.

"No, we're deciding on whether to work our way south or north. There's a critical need to focus on the Cumberland and Tennessee River watershed since their spring floods decimated those areas, too," he said.

While Amy continued her questioning, the idea of his eventual departure from town kept pushing its way to the forefront of his mind. The notion of leaving Port Chance had weighed heavily on him, especially since the bonfire. He'd come here knowing his stay wouldn't be permanent. His altruistic sense of helping inspired his mission, but seeing Kit again did, too. And while they'd become friendly again, she still held back.

Focus.

Every other thought literally conjured up Kit's image.

The interview continued for another half hour. He talked Amy into trying a piece of the Dutch apple pie. She declared it a slice of "true Americana," and thanked him for his time. After they parted ways a short time later, Holden headed toward Love's Landing. Kit's truck was parked in its usual spot, but the *Dolly Swain* was already gone.

Holden pulled into the spot next to Kit's truck. He got out, zipping his coat against the unseasonably frigid air, and stuffed his hands in his pockets. His breath puffed out in short spurts.

What kind of group would get on a boat in this weather?

He chuckled to himself as soon as the thought popped into his head.

A number of groups wouldn't blink at getting outside in temperatures like this. Hiking clubs, nature groups, people who preferred winter over the sweltering, humidity-drenched air of an Iowan summer.

He and Kit were alike that way.

His boots scuffed along the pavement as he walked the length of chain-link fence that ran parallel to the sidewalk. The fence had stretched all the way down to the end of the parking area when he was in high school, maybe a hundred feet long or more. Now, just this shorter section remained.

Squatting, he studied the locks dangling from the fence. He grasped a red one, studying the initials, feeling the cold metal bite into his skin. It was a newer addition to the fence, judging by the rough edges of the letters carved with an engraver's pick or knife.

He sighed and stood again.

Hundreds of locks washed away in the flood. Now only a few dozen remained. Yet someone had erected a new sign here, explaining the story about getting "locked" on Love's Landing, a tradition in Port Chance. His parents had placed a lock here. So had his aunt and uncle. It'd been a thing in high school to walk down to the river and ask a girl if she wanted to get locked. Maybe the guy already held one in his pocket, carved and ready to add to the fence if she said yes. Or, if he wasn't feeling lucky, they'd pick out a lock together after the fact at the hardware store or find an old but clean one at John Goodwin's antique shop.

Holden dropped his chin into the warm folds of his coat and rested his arms over the top rail of the fence as he gazed out across the river.

He'd never added a lock to the fence, not that he hadn't tried.

He'd pitched it into the river after Kit turned him down. What good would it have done to keep it? Now it lay buried beneath layers of silt and rock, a proper burial place for it and his feelings for her.

Yet here you are.

Maybe the lock wasn't even in Port Chance anymore, carried downstream by storms and the currents from watercraft.

The forlorn sound of a boat horn echoed in the distance. Closer still, the heavy machinery grinded near the site for the new Yellow Pier Restaurant. He'd sat at the café counter at Mowdry's Market just that morning within full view of the construction activity. While he nibbled on a fresh-baked cinnamon scone, he listened to a group of older men buzzing about when their old haunt would be ready again to welcome them back.

Some things never changed. He wished that had been the case with him and Kit. He'd go back in time in a heartbeat if he could change the trajectory of his and Kit's story.

His phone buzzed in his pocket, a message from Portia.

The crew is on track to get the barge up here by the end of next week. Weather looks okay on both ends.

He thrust out another breath.

Now to tell Kit.

Chapter Eighteen

K it waited in her truck for Holden to appear outside his front door just as the sun blazed over the horizon the next morning. He held two insulated cups when he showed his face a few minutes later, one for her and one for him, as he sauntered down the driveway. The brown canvas coat with the leather collar he wore looked amazing on him. Kit tried hard not to stare as he approached her car.

"This is my favorite blend from the roastery down near Quincy. Try it," he said, thrusting a cup toward her as soon as he hopped into the passenger seat.

She thanked him for the proffered cup, sipped, and confirmed with a nod that it tasted decent. Her gaze glided over him. As discreet as she thought she was, Holden caught her.

"Better than Daily Grind?" he asked with a smirk.

"Why do I have to choose?"

He shrugged. "I just thought you'd have an opinion."

"I'm never short on opinions, but I don't always feel like sharing."

"Fair enough," he said.

She pulled out of her driveway and headed up to the main highway which would take them to Furever Friends Rescue and Rehab, twenty minutes outside of town.

She'd slept in spurts last night, jolting awake like she'd been poked with a branding iron each time. When Holden called the night before to ask if today might be a good time to help Sadie at the shelter, she hadn't hesitated to agree. But it cost her a restful night. As much as she wanted to be near Holden, she fretted about becoming too attached. She'd felt off-kilter since the bonfire. The dynamic had changed between them, not that it was her doing. It left her unsettled and unable to get a solid night's sleep. Her mood bordered between mildly irritated and bona fide crab at the moment, and being forced to diss Daily Grind, no matter how sublime this Quincy brew tasted, wasn't going to improve her temperament.

"What time do you have to be back to the office?" she asked a couple minutes into the drive. Holden held his phone in one hand and the coffee cup in the other, reading something.

"Oh, you know. Whenever," he said distractedly.

"You have nothing on your agenda today?" He still hadn't secured all of the permits for the cleanup to begin. She kept quiet and didn't want to probe him about it. The longer this process took, the better it looked for her tour season to end without a hitch.

That got his attention. He dropped his phone into his lap.

"I do. Nothing pressing, though," he said toward his window. "Maybe we could get lunch after this?"

She shook her head before he finished the sentence.

"No can do. Full schedule today. I shouldn't even be going to Sadie's right now."

"We could have found another time." His tone said otherwise. The excitement in his voice when he called the night before to arrange this had been obvious.

"No, I'd rather have this behind me."

She caught him studying her with his lips folded shut.

"What?" she asked.

He settled back and looked straight ahead. "Nothing. I just thought we could make a day of this."

"This isn't a date, Holden."

"I didn't say it was." He paused before he looked at her again. "Listen, it sounds like the barge will show up by the end of next week."

Kit stared at the road in silence, but the gears in her head went from zero to one hundred in less time than it takes a Mustang GT to reach its top speed.

"So, will I be able to keep the tours on my schedule or not?" She tried to keep the edginess from her tone, but didn't have any luck.

"My crew leader and I will meet later today to talk about positioning it along the shoreline. I'm really hoping your tours won't be affected."

"You and me both," she said sarcastically. Then in a whisper, she added, "Please don't make me cancel them."

Silence filled the rest of the drive. Her mind spun with scenarios of breaking the news to her clients that she had to cancel their booking.

They pulled into the dirt drive that twisted its way through a shallow stand of trees and past the newly erected sanctuary sign that their father had installed just last week. Having renovated a tired old Cape Cod and its handful of outbuildings into a sanctuary property and medical facility shortly after college,

Sadie had nurtured Furever Friends from the ground up. She wasn't as talented in the construction trades as Kit, but under the tutelage of Aaron Wendell, each of his girls could hold their own doing basic repairs, including Sadie. As a new homeowner, she'd found the house to be an ongoing project, one with constant needs.

Sadie stood next to a wire cage on the back of a maroon pickup as they parked nearby. An elderly couple stood by, watching.

"Who's this?" Kit asked when she and Holden met Sadie at the truck. A raccoon with an open wound on its back paced inside the cage, hissing and baring its teeth.

"New patient. Some head trauma, too. Hit by a car most likely," Sadie said as she heaved the cage from the tailgate.

"Thank you for taking it in. My wife can't drive by an animal on the road without checking if it's still alive," said the man. His wife acknowledged the truth of his words with a nod while she wrote out a check.

"For the good work you do," the woman said as she handed the check to Sadie.

"Thank you," said Sadie. "And I'm glad you spotted this little gal. She should be up and running again in no time after some TLC."

The man and his wife climbed back into their truck and left while Sadie carried the cage toward the building next to the house.

"Can I help?" Holden offered to take the cage from her, but Sadie twisted away.

"Thanks, but no. Not unless you have results from a recent TB test."

Holden shook his head as he fell into step with Kit again.

They followed Sadie into the building, a large shed converted into an intake room and lined with cages and tanks of all sizes. Some of the larger cages connected to wire-enclosed runs outside, separated by insulated, remote-controlled doors.

Holden stood in the middle of the room, taking in the variety of patients Sadie cared for at the moment. Raccoons, squirrels, a mink, and one very perturbed fox.

"That's Chester," Sadie said to Holden, who looked visibly tense. "So far he's not too appreciative of what I've done to make him comfortable here."

Holden swallowed. "I'm sure he'll come around."

"They don't usually, and that's a good thing," said Sadie. "We don't want to treat the wild right out of them."

"Of course not." Holden stepped toward the cage for a closer look at Chester. The fox crouched, revealing two rows of needle teeth as his lips peeled back.

Sadie donned thick leather gloves that reached her elbows. She lifted the sliding door with one hand while she blocked the opening with the other. No sooner had she reached into the cage and pulled out the raccoon than it rested on the examination table, calm and quiet.

"Thanks for coming out, you guys," Sadie said as she studied the animal's skin underneath its thick coat for other signs of trauma. "I try not to take advantage too much. It makes me feel guilty. But between these guys coming in at all hours and my lack of funds half the time, it's impossible to hire the work to get finished."

"You're not taking advantage of anyone. We're happy to help..." His voice trailed off as he fixed Kit with a sideways smile. "Right?"

"Of course," she answered. Warmth flushed her face. It was sweet of him, taking time to help her sister.

"I'm going to get my tool box," he said.

"Can you grab mine, too?"

"I like how he includes himself in our family things," mused Sadie when the door closed behind him. "How do you feel about that?"

"Oh, I don't know. He's leaving eventually, so I try not to read too much into what he says and does." Holden's time in Port Chance was winding down, especially since he now knew when to expect the barge. She tried to push it out of her mind for the time being.

Sadie cast a quick glance at Holden's back through the front window.

"Wouldn't it be cool if he stayed—"

That fruitless thought had played on repeat in her head since Holden appeared on her dock.

"He won't," she said with a sigh.

Throughout the morning, Holden worked on the plumbing issues in the cabin while Kit changed out an outlet in the intake room and installed a ceiling fan. Then they switched locations. While she added two outlets to the bedroom and a light switch in the cabin, the scurry of mice inside the walls made her keep an eye on the floor near her feet. Unless Sadie's new rehab partner didn't mind furry roommates, Sadie needed a cat in here, *pronto*.

After she repacked her tool box, she went in search of Holden. Two hours had flown by; she needed to get back to town. She found him applying glue to new PVC underneath a sink in the intake room. Sadie had the raccoon out of the cage again, holding her down with one gloved hand while she administered something in a syringe into its mouth. They were deep in conversation about rescue work when Kit settled into a chair to wait for Holden to finish.

"Most of the raccoon babies that come in are with me for weeks, sometimes months. I do what's called soft releases when they're ready."

"What's that?" Holden asked. He sat up from lying on his side to apply more glue to the PVC.

Sadie set the empty syringe on the towel, then picked up the raccoon by the scruff of her neck and supported her bottom with the other hand. She pushed her gently into a large, clean cage against the wall, then fastened the door. The raccoon snuffled around in the straw, checking out her new digs while keeping one eye on her audience.

"Basically, I release them close by and keep food and shelter available for them to come and go as they please. It's an easier transition for the young ones that way."

"But they eventually all leave?" Holden asked.

"Almost always," Kit answered for Sadie. She'd always been fascinated by the raccoons, probably because those were what Sadie saw the most of in her rescue work. "They're wild. They aren't meant to be held back."

"If they're handed all the things they need to survive, why not come back though?" His gaze locked on hers.

"That's not their nature," she answered without pause. "Maybe they'll show up every now and again, but eventually they leave. For good."

"But they know where home is."

Kit squared her shoulders. "Home is out there. Not here."

Sadie's eyes darted between them as if they spoke a language she didn't understand. Meanwhile, Holden quietly gave in, and when Kit met his eyes again, his expression had clouded over.

Back in the truck a short time later, Holden's silence filled the cab. It'd been a productive, if awkward, morning. They left Sadie's having finished what they came to do. That was most important.

They pulled into Kit's driveway, and Holden's hand was on the door when he spoke.

"You said something in the coffee shop last week. That I keep taking," he said, hooking his fingers in the air while emphasizing the last word. "But you never told me what that meant."

"I don't remember what point I was making." She shook her head for emphasis. Not that she didn't know, she just didn't want to open that wound again. They'd come to an agreement since then. Their friendship, while tenuous, was reestablished. Nothing more, nothing less.

"Thanks for letting me tag along," he said.

She swallowed. The second she met his gaze, a slow grin transformed his features.

"I'm glad you did. I'll be waiting to hear about your clean-up schedule." In the meantime, she'd cross her fingers that something would delay Holden's barge yet again.

"We make a good team. Maybe we should take our gig on the road."

She couldn't hold back the smile. "HGTV meets *Friends*."

"I'd watch that," he said.

Kit caught herself lingering on the gentle curve of his mouth and the way his cheeks plumped up when he smiled. She almost reached out to smooth the stray curl that fell over his eye, but caught herself.

"Me too."

He reached for his tool box at his feet as he left her truck, but he leaned inside instead of closing the door.

"Do you ever think about how much we have in common?"

"I...maybe...I used to." Her face flushed. She focused on unbuckling the seatbelt, so he wouldn't notice, but her fingers fumbled on the release.

"Sometimes I wonder why we never connected, you know, that way."

She looked up at him, trying to link two words together for a response, but her brain betrayed her. It was empty, void of all coherent thought.

Nothing. Nada. Zip.

"Sorry, I didn't mean to say that. Just thinking out loud, I guess," he added. "It's just strange, you know?"

If Holden couldn't see her pulse rippling in her neck, he was blind. She pulled her collar close to her chin.

And why is he thinking this now, and not twenty years ago?

Holden's expression melted into embarrassment when she stayed quiet. His eyes widened as he looked away. He placed a hand on his throat as if he had trouble swallowing. She'd almost feel sorry for him if she wasn't still recovering from the shock.

"Anyway, I...uh, take care," he said hurriedly before he stalked across the driveway to his front door.

Don't go.

She almost called out to him, but it was like one of those dreams where danger loomed and she stood frozen.

She blinked as two words formed on the tip of her tongue.

But all that she managed to say was "You, too."

Chapter Nineteen

Later that afternoon, Holden and his crew leader, Erin, stood over a map on the long oak table in his office, studying the shoreline topography along Port Chance.

"I don't see how we can park the barge anywhere other than in this area," said Erin, tracing the spot around Kit's dock with her finger. "There's too much of a buildup along the banks to chance us bottoming out."

Holden suspected as much, though he'd hoped to avoid closing Kit down for a few days. He'd hated leaving her in limbo that morning until he consulted with Erin, who'd used sonar to detect obstacles below the surface—standard procedure when they worked in new locations.

At the door, Portia cleared her throat.

"Given the conversation you're having at the moment, I thought I'd let you know that Kit woman called," Portia said with a barely contained eye roll. "You know, in case you need to call her back ASAP."

"Yeah?" His voice hitched, so he cleared his throat. "Did she leave a message?"

"I'll say." She picked up the yellow slip of paper. "'Could use your help. Bring your appetite and be at the boat before sunset. There will be pie.'" She looked at him over the top of her glasses. "Are you sure you know what you're getting yourself into, Boss?"

"She left that?" His face flushed. Was Kit finally coming around? He was shocked to hear from her so soon after their awkward parting.

"Sure did."

"Yes, I know what I'm up against. She's a hornet-turned-honey-bee once you get to know her." Maybe he should up the game. Bring a bottle of wine, candles for a little atmosphere.

"Honey bees sting, too."

He chuckled. "Not if you know how to handle them." Forget the wine and candles. Kit would laugh him out of town. This required a little creativity.

Portia rolled her eyes again and went back to typing. "If you say so."

He finished planning with Erin, then settled into his chair and kicked his feet up on the desk, preparing to text Kit back. But as his finger hovered over his phone's keypad, he second-guessed himself.

What if I just show up?

Her message *had* invited him to do just that.

He tossed his phone on the desk, his mind whirling. He hoped to soften the blow of his news a bit. He didn't want to crush her, but it almost sounded like Kit had come to terms with the possibility.

Outside, the sun floated above the river, a reddish-orange

orb. In another hour it would be tipping the trees on the horizon. He couldn't wait until then.

Shrugging on his coat, Holden hurried past a bewildered Portia.

"Heading out for the day. I'll see you tomorrow morning."

Portia huffed, not taking her eyes from the monitor on her desk.

"Watch that stinger, Boss."

"Thanks for your concern, Portia."

Kit unloaded boxes from the *Dolly Swain* onto the pier when Holden pulled into the parking space near the landing. She saw him, waved, then went back to shifting boxes on deck.

His heart crouched at the back of his throat, threatening to render him mute if he tried to speak. That was probably a good thing, considering his mindless comments earlier when he asked if she'd ever wondered about them as a couple.

He almost buried his face in his shirt collar thinking about it again.

What an idiot I am.

"Can I help?" he called when he got closer.

She straightened, rubbing a spot on her back. "Nah, almost finished packing up. But I could use help getting them into my truck."

"What is this stuff?" Upon closer inspection, a half dozen plastic totes surrounded Kit. Another dozen were already stacked on the pier.

"Just offloading some supplies that I use for the tours since I'll be slowing down soon."

He nodded, feeling the tension spring into his shoulders again at the thought of bringing up just how soon she'd be closing up shop.

"I take it you got my message," she said, her voice strained as she hoisted a box and made her way to the gate.

"I did." He reached for the box, and she willingly handed it over without a fuss. Their hands brushed, and he felt the tingle of contact. He glanced at Kit, but her eyes had already darted away.

"I wasn't confident Portia would pass that along. She's not a fan," Kit said with a small smile.

He chuckled. Kit hadn't managed to endear herself to his office assistant since their first meeting. Knowing Kit, she didn't dwell on it.

"She's slow to warm up to people." He set the box next to the others on the pier, then climbed aboard.

"Especially ones who stand up to her."

"Yes, that."

"Anyway, the River City Ornithology Club isn't big on snacking when they're birdwatching. They ordered the deluxe brown bag lunches for the group, including two of Monte's pies," she said, sweeping an arm toward the large box of brown sack lunches lined up on the bench as well as the two cream-topped pies sitting next to them. "Only half of the group touched the lunches. Then they forgot to take them."

"Their loss is your gain." He peeked into one of the bags.

"Your gain, too. I can't eat all this by myself," she said. "Do you want to take some back for your office staff?"

"I could..." Maybe she'd second-guessed herself about the message she left with Portia, the part about bringing his appetite.

"I just refilled my thermos at Daily Grind," she said, still not looking at him. "We could finish off one of these bags if you want before you help me load. And I know you can't resist one of Monte's pies."

There we go.

He reached inside his coat pocket and brought out the object he'd been waiting to show her since the last time she mentioned pie.

"Is that...?" Her brows arced in surprise.

"The one and only."

She took his Nana's silver pie server, a wistful grin softening her expression.

"I loved this thing."

"She passed it down to me last Thanksgiving."

She turned it over in her hand, tracing the etched design on the triangular head of the server with a fingertip.

"I never got tired of hearing Nana repeat its history," she murmured.

"I know."

Kit had loved the story about his great-grandfather finding it in a little French town near Cantigny during World War I, then bringing it back for his wife after the armistice was signed. The etchings depicted a couple caring for their farm animals with a barn and forest as a backdrop, and fleurs-de-lis ringed the handle. Time had blurred the sharpness of the engravings, but it was no less charming.

"It's like holding a piece of my childhood." When she looked up at him, her eyes looked moist. "Does it still cut pie, or have you retired it?"

"I'm pretty sure it still works."

She gave him a decisive nod. "Let's find out."

Chapter Twenty

Despite the chilled air, Kit unzipped her coat to cool off from the exertion of packing and moving boxes. She set the box of lunches at their feet and sat down on the bench, patting the seat next to her. Holden wasted no time taking her up on the offer.

"You're wearing the sweatshirt," he said with an amused look.

She looked down at herself and shrugged. The Port Chance Pickles sweatshirt he'd bought for her on his first day back in town was still hideous.

"It's warm. The color is terrible, but I'm a practical girl."

She dug into one of the bags at her feet, unwrapping a ham sandwich. She offered him one half, then poured some of the coffee from her thermos into a Styrofoam cup, and she handed that over, too. They ate in silence for a while, listening to the birds which flocked to the grassy point in the state park a short distance away to the north.

When it came time for pie, he took the server from the bench between them and sliced into the creamy topping after she popped off the plastic lid. Again, they ate in silence, only exchanging smiles. All she could think about was how this moment echoed so many similar ones from their past. The memories smoldered inside Kit, chasing away the chilly November air. She wondered if the same sentiments swirled around in Holden's mind. She bet they did, judging by the way he kept sneaking looks at her.

"What's on your mind?" she asked after a while, hoping she wouldn't regret it.

His chest rose and fell. "I've been trying to think of a way to bring it up."

"You know I'm not the beat-around-the-bush kind of girl." She held her breath, anticipation rushing through her body. Would this be another admission like he'd shared that morning? This time she'd be ready.

"I know," he said.

Impatience got the best of her. "Just say it."

His gaze dipped downward. He set his empty plate beside him on the bench.

"About the barge. We'll likely have to drop anchor close to Love's Landing."

"I can work around it, right?" She didn't like the sick look on his face.

"I don't think you understand the scope..."

"Can you just say it?"

"It'll be hard to move your boat once we're anchored."

"How hard?"

His chest rose and fell with a deep breath.

"Impossible."

Kit looked up at him, clamping down so hard on her lip that it hurt.

"So I'll have to cancel the scheduled tours?"

She wanted him to say it. It was part of his punishment. He deserved it.

He nodded again.

"Yes. I'm so sorry." He grimaced while his chin dropped to his chest. "I'll make it up to you, Kit. I promise."

Whether to yell or cry, Kit couldn't decide.

"I think I need to be alone," she said instead.

Holden laid a hand on her arm, not meeting her eyes. Under better circumstances, his touch would have ignited her senses, the way he rubbed the spot as if trying to soothe her. It was a tender, heartfelt gesture filled with longing. But when he curled his hand into a fist and dropped it at his side after a few moments, hurt replaced the brief pleasure of his touch.

He dumped his plate into the plastic garbage bag at their feet and carried the box with the remaining lunches to his truck.

She stayed put on the cushioned bench, wondering if he'd turn back to continue the conversation, but honestly, she couldn't bear to listen to another word. Instead, Holden climbed into his truck and sat behind the steering wheel. Even at this distance, pain registered on his face. Deep lines punctuated the corners of his mouth as he frowned.

So what?

She was done. Holden had steered the course of their relationship for far too long. It was time to put him behind her again and look forward. Nothing from their past would ever interfere with her or her heart again.

Chapter Twenty-One

Five days later, Holden directed the EcoPartners crew to position their barge near Love's Landing, and then they got to work. By noon the first day, they'd hauled two tons of debris away from the river bank. The local volunteer group that Dan and Portia had organized through social media was a force. Erin half-jokingly remarked they should all be hired permanently.

The *Dolly Swain* rested quietly against the pier. Of course the weather cooperated perfectly for the cleanup—blue skies, no wind, and temperatures hitting the upper fifties. Holden's guilt hit the stratosphere. These last few days of ideal weather would have been a perfect endnote to Kit's tour season. She'd occupied his thoughts constantly since they parted ways on the boat.

He'd called her fruitlessly, but Kit had refused his calls. He'd sent a courier to her house with a certified check, at least wanting to compensate her for the lost business. So far, she hadn't acknowledged it was received, and it did little to alleviate his guilt.

On the third day of the scheduled cleanup, Holden strolled into downtown Port Chance on his lunch break. He stopped to talk to Mayor Jarvis, who asked about his parents, as she left Daisy Gap Café. He also ran into Thomas Hicklebourne, the owner of the Yellow Pier Restaurant, too, and talked with him about the progress on rebuilding. His grand reopening was set for February, just in time for Valentine's Day.

The Lorches' new storefront bakery seemed to be getting plenty of traffic up ahead. He paused at the door while customers left the shop with pink boxes in hand. The last person held the door for him so he stepped over the threshold and breathed in the sweet scent of cinnamon and yeast.

"Holden!"

Rose hurried from behind the counter to give him a hug. "What brings you by?"

"Sweets, of course." He grinned when Rose reached for the glass-covered platter behind her and took the lid off. She waved dessert samples under his nose.

"Care for a pumpkin cream cheese bar or something else?" she asked. "The pumpkin bar is a new recipe, so I need feedback."

Choosing just one of Rose's creations was a real dilemma. Next to the pumpkin bars, a frosted brownie sample loaded with nuts and chocolate chunks called his name. She sensed his indecision.

"Take two samples," she said. "That's what they're here for."

"Amazing," he said around a mouthful. "I'll take a half dozen cinnamon rolls, too."

"You got it," she said, replacing the glass cover.

"I also need a piece of advice."

She froze, her eyes wide. "Of course. That'll cost you extra, though."

He nodded with a smile, formulating the question in his head so it didn't come out as too intrusive. Rose set the platter back on the counter, boxed up his cinnamon rolls, then pointed to one of the tables against the wall.

"What's going on?" she asked when they were seated.

Rose had always felt like an older sister. Calm, authoritative. Always able to settle the storms Janie and Kit set in motion. Kit had once told him that Rose was the one person Kit looked to when she felt misunderstood by everyone else.

"I hope I'm not out of line bringing this up," he started, and was immediately comforted by Rose's steady hand on top of his own.

"You're like family, Holden. Whatever it is, don't worry about it."

"It's Kit."

Rose's expression softened, the worry lines on her forehead smoothed over with understanding.

"Of course it is," she said with a chuckle.

"I'm wondering if it was a mistake coming back here. Trying to reconnect with her." He'd turned this question over in his mind since showing up on her dock almost two months ago. So far, a solid answer had escaped him. "When I think we're making headway, something sets her off and she shuts down."

Rose sighed and looked at the ceiling. "So typical. I'm not sure where that comes from. I don't remember her being this guarded when we were younger. She was actually the most affectionate of us four, the most demonstrative." She paused. "Don't you remember that?"

"I do."

She'd always clutched his arm when she had something to confide or a joke to share. The friendly nudges and punches had always been a part of Kit's dynamic energy. He'd fallen under her spell early, sometime around the time when their parents worked closely together on rebuilding Good Shepherd Methodist Church, when they were eight or nine years old. They'd spent a lot of time together, playing around the church grounds while the congregation salvaged what had survived an electrical fire, then throughout the planning, building, and moving into the new church, too. He and Kit had shared a love of romping in the wooded ravines near the Huckleberry River, and baseball, of course. He'd practiced his pitching with Kit when they joined the local youth team during that same summer, ignoring his friends' teasing until they discovered she could out throw, out run, and out hit any one of them.

"Do you think...when I left town..."

"That it hurt her? Definitely." Rose lifted a shoulder, glancing toward the door when a couple entered the shop. "She never would have confided that in me, though. Definitely not back then."

He nodded thoughtfully, pondering his situation. How much longer should he spend in Port Chance, hoping she'd come around? He could wrap up his time in town as soon as next week. That was four days away.

"Here's the thing about Kit," Rose started. "She's fiercely loyal until she has a reason not to be. You leaving town, the *way* you left town, broke something in her. I'm not saying it's not fixable. It's just...well, you know Kit. She's a puzzle most of the time."

Holden knew something happened well before he left Port Chance, though.

The dynamics of their friendship had shifted in high school. They remained close, but Kit grew more standoffish. Moody. He remembered the day when she'd shocked him by showing up to school in a skirt freshman year. It'd been picture day, so everyone tended to dress nicer anyway. But when Kit hopped on the bus that morning and sat beside him, he'd laughed nervously. He'd made a big deal of it like an idiot, and everyone around them chuckled along with him. He'd never forget the crushing embarrassment that had lit her cheeks on fire. Or her fierce scowl that followed him for days afterward. He'd breeched the trusted bond between them. Maybe that had been the start of Kit's withdrawal.

The bells above the door jingled again as another handful of shoppers came inside. Rose squeezed his hand.

"I don't have to tell you to be patient. You know that girl better than anyone," she said.

Maybe he did, and that was what worried him. Her indifference might be a sign that she wasn't willing to risk her heart again. For friendship or anything more.

He chuckled. "Will that work in my favor or lead to my demise? That's the question of the hour."

"I probably gave you more things to worry about than answers," said Rose.

"No, it was helpful."

"I'm glad you came in. You can talk to me anytime."

"Thanks, Rose. I appreciate it." He stood.

She gave him a parting hug and an affectionate pat on the cheek.

As he walked toward the door, he paused next to it. The sign caught his eye.

Fill a Bag. Get a Bag.

A small pyramid of rolled garbage bags, each tied with a pink polka dot ribbon, rested next to one of Rose's pastry bags.

He turned toward Rose again. "What's this?"

Rose grinned. "You and Kit didn't cook this up together?"

He shook his head, confused.

"Well, then." Rose's grin broadened. "This might be her way of moving forward."

"I don't get it."

"She came up with the idea to give away donuts when anyone takes a garbage bag and fills it with litter around town." She handed him the printed postcard explaining the promotion's details. "She brought these in a couple weeks ago. Made this herself. People have been texting me photos of garbage bags since the weekend. I had to give Trudy extra hours to keep up with the free donuts we've given away."

The gesture made him momentarily speechless.

"It surprised me, too. Kit's never been one to initiate something like this. I think you've inspired her."

"I'll be..."

Rose snickered. "I know. In Kitspeak, this is huge."

Chapter Twenty-Two

Reluctantly, Kit had made three calls the night after Holden told her about his company's clean-up schedule, pushing the tasks off until the last minute as she halfheartedly hoped Holden would call her back.

I'm cancelling the whole project, he'd say.

Maybe he couldn't get a volunteer crew together.

Or the garbage barge had capsized on the uneven river bottom somewhere. Wishful thinking, except for the barge scenario. She'd felt guilty when that thought crossed her mind.

Cancelling the tours for the history club, the Hermitage Hiking and Outdoor Club, and the Polar Express boat-themed birthday party for an acquaintance of Rose's cut her deeply, though. She'd scrambled all spring and summer to fill out her calendar.

When Holden let her know the timeline for EcoPartners' work near her dock, his tone had been clipped. He'd apologized, but she still tasted bitterness in the whole situation, even with the lingering sweetness still in her mouth from the pie they'd shared on the *Dolly Swain*.

Now, she crossed the parking lot of the market, her arms loaded with two grocery bags of food for the Wendell Thanksgiving tomorrow. She walked a wide circle around Mona Jarvis and a woman Kit only knew as Vera, who stood in her way, looking toward the river. Mona spotted her and managed to stop her anyway.

"That's quite the garbage barge," Mona said in her characteristic boom of a voice. "Kit, I hope that didn't affect business. You're finished with tours for the year, right?"

She didn't feel like rehashing how Holden's company had quashed the end of her season just days ago.

"I am."

"What a monstrosity," Vera said as Kit spotted the barge on the river that'd stopped them in their tracks. The dread she'd felt canceling the tours lifted a moment as the enormity of Holden's mission floated into view.

"Holden Berne sure has taken it upon himself to clean up this town," Vera added.

"And I can't thank him enough," Mona said. "It's a wonderful contribution to his hometown."

"But it's going to interfere with the holiday boat parade," Vera countered. She owned property on the river and threw a big bash on parade day every year.

"It'll be long gone by then," Kit said. As mad as she was about the intrusion, she didn't like listening to someone criticize Holden.

The woman wandered off, shaking her head.

"I knew Holden's venture would get the town buzzing when that reporter showed up at city hall," Mona said. "Did she happen to talk to you, too?"

"Reporter? No, I haven't talked to anyone."

Mona flapped her shopping list toward Holden's barge. "A little positive publicity never hurts. If you see him, tell him we appreciate him and his crew. Maybe I'll round up some people to host a little thank-you celebration. Think he'd like that?"

Kit nodded, distracted. "I'm sure he would."

"I'll get on that. Nice to see you, Kit. Happy Thanksgiving to the Wendell clan," Mona said, waving her shopping list in her direction.

She kept her eye on the barge as she pulled out of the market's parking lot and made her way through town. It disappeared behind the wooded area near the state park, then appeared again for an instant as she drove up the hill toward her parents' place.

A part of her chest had felt hollowed out since Holden left her on the *Dolly Swain* last week. She'd fought the urge to go out onto her deck when he and Sarge were outside these last few days. All that needed to be said had been spoken, but the feeling of unfinished business plagued her. Maybe it had something to do with the certified check from EcoPartners showing up on her doorstep, his attempt to make up for the cancelled tours. Melancholy replaced her anger at him shutting down her tours. She'd grown so accustomed to Holden's presence again, knowing he was just a few steps away from her door to his, that the silence between them seemed loud. *Too* loud.

A few minutes later, she unloaded the grocery bags onto her parents' kitchen counter. The room was overly warm with the sun glinting through the multi-paned picture window over the kitchen table. In preparation for tomorrow, Janie and their mother had been prepping food for half the day. Their chatter filled the kitchen with a cheerful prelude to the holiday. Kit rummaged through the cabinets to find a casserole dish to hold her cranberry relish recipe, half-listening to their conversation.

"What's Holden doing for Thanksgiving?" Janie asked.

Kit almost dropped the dish in her hand as she closed the cabinet door.

"How should I know?"

Her tone came out more brusque than she intended. She gritted her teeth, keeping her eye on the food items she sorted through on the counter.

"Sorry, didn't mean for that to come out the way it did," she mumbled.

She chanced a look at her mother as Janie and Sonya exchanged glances.

Holden hadn't mentioned specific plans when she'd shared that her Thanksgiving involved a gathering big enough that her father cleaned out the garage every November to accommodate their extended family. They expected close to forty people tomorrow. All Holden had said was that he'd head out of town. Either he didn't have Thanksgiving plans or he didn't want to share them.

"Maybe we should have extended an invitation to him," Janie said.

"I don't think so." She set an apple onto the cutting board and chopped it in half with gusto. Beside her, Janie jumped.

Sonya set down her potato peeler and faced her. "What's the problem, Kit?"

She narrowly missed her thumb with the knife as she set to dicing one half of the apple.

"Not a thing."

"It's Holden," Janie said matter-of-factly. "You said his name."

Kit set the knife down. "Okay, here's the problem. I keep asking myself the same question, and I can't come up with an answer."

"What question is that?" her mother asked.

"Why does everyone keep trying to push us together since he came back to town?"

"It's not like that, Kit," Sonya said.

"No? It sure feels that way." His absence cut deeper with everyone pointing it out.

Janie draped an arm around her shoulder.

"I, for one, was excited to see him back in town. He was like family when we were growing up," she said.

"Well, things have changed," she said. She hadn't told anyone about how Holden's clean-up mission had affected the last week of her season, and she wanted to keep it that way. All it took was a drive past Love's Landing to know anyway. Either they hadn't a clue, or her family was considerate enough not to mention it.

"As things always do," Sonya added. "Rose told us that her friend's birthday party for her daughter was cancelled because of Holden's project. I know how that must have hurt."

Kit looked up at the ceiling and groaned. Sometimes she really didn't like living in a small town.

"I don't think he intentionally wanted to hurt you," Sonya continued. "That's not Holden at all. Your tours coinciding with the cleanup was—"

"Collateral damage," Janie blurted. "Just forgive him, Kit. It's easiest that way."

"Yeah? For who?"

Janie stepped closer and tapped on Kit's temple. "Your brain will thank you."

She'd always struggled with the forgiveness part—back then and now. She'd also started to believe Holden hadn't acted maliciously, leaving town without a word all those years ago. But somehow that felt even worse, like their friendship was so inconsequential that she hadn't deserved a goodbye.

Now, as he wrapped up his work in Port Chance, at least until spring, he'd head home again. Maybe he'd already left. His crew could finish here without him. He'd said so himself. It felt like the summer of her senior year all over again. One day he was here, the next day—*poof!* Gone.

"Besides, wouldn't it feel better to part ways on good terms this time?" Janie asked.

She threw a scowl in Janie's direction before she focused on dicing the apple again. That was easier said than done, not that Janie knew Kit's feelings for Holden.

"We're more alike than you care to admit, Sis. I felt the same way when Mark and I split up."

"Oh, yeah? How so?" Maybe if she'd acknowledge Janie instead of trying to ignore her, she'd stop talking.

"It was so much safer to fight the battle in my own mind instead of confronting it head on. I was too scared. I should have chased him down and settled it sooner. *Demanded* it be settled."

Their mother clucked her tongue at Janie. "Three years was a long time to come to that realization, dear."

"Right? Thank goodness I came to my senses." She wiggled her left hand to show off the ring. "And now look at us."

She couldn't imagine Janie being intimidated by anything. They were at least alike *that* way.

Kit chuckled. "What were *you* scared of?"

"Of him maybe telling me that we were finished. For good,"

Janie said. She shook her shoulders as if ridding herself of a bad memory. "Again, I'd conjured this whole frightening scenario in my head. Turns out he was afraid of the same things."

Kit used the knife to scrape apple pieces from the cutting board into the mixing bowl as her thoughts rested firmly on the past week. Holden was always the one leaving, not her.

But chase him down like Janie did with Mark? Not a chance.

Chapter Twenty-Three

Holden and his father, Buck Berne, rested their heels on the metal railing of the deck overlooking the river. He'd made the three-hour trip to stay at his parents' home in Hannibal the night before. His grandparents, along with his mother, brother, and his brother's family had joined them for the day. The others prepped the Thanksgiving meal inside while Holden and his father talked outside, away from the mingled voices in the house.

Behind them, the smoker emitted the mouth-watering aroma of turkey which had been roasting since early morning. The sun warmed their faces as they talked about Holden's work up north. Throughout their conversation, Kit's face flashed in his mind as he wondered what she was doing at that moment. That she might be looking at the same river in Port Chance satisfied him. A connection, even if they were two hundred miles apart.

"This is a fine article," Buck said as he finished reading the copy of the *River City Times* that Holden had brought home for his parents to read. Amy Warre's article with his interview had published a few days ago. He set the folded newspaper on the table between them. "I bet the folks in Port Chance were especially thankful one of their own had a hand in this."

"They were. I've heard from quite a few people. We're not finished yet. We'll be back in the spring."

"We don't make it up there as much as we like," Buck mused. "Can't say I miss living up there. Winters were brutal. But we left plenty of good friends behind."

"Have you had much contact with the Wendells over the years?"

Buck eyed him. "Some. Why?"

"No reason."

Buck looked toward the river again with a grin spreading across his face. "That rental you're in. Kit lives next door, doesn't she?"

He nodded. The Wheelers, long-time friends of his parents, cut him a deal on a month-to-month lease.

"How's that working out?" Buck asked.

He shrugged. "Fine."

"Your mother always thought you two would end up together."

This was news. "Really?"

His father nodded. "Can't say I thought about it either way, but I always liked having her around. Smart as a whip, that one. A spitfire."

The patio door slid open behind them a few minutes later. His mother, Faith, wrapped a sweater around her shoulders as she joined them.

"Dinner is in an hour," she said. "That turkey should probably come out soon."

Buck looked over his shoulder and nodded. "Hey, didn't you think Holden and Kit Wendell would end up together?"

His mother snorted. "Now that's a random question. What brought that up?"

Holden squirmed in his chair. "We've been talking about my work in Port Chance. Dad mentioned it."

Faith hugged her chest. "I think I do remember saying that. You two spent so much time together."

"We had a lot in common is all."

Faith came around the chairs to lean against the railing, facing them. "Maybe so, but I remember the way she looked at you."

"What do you mean?"

"She worshipped you."

He laughed. "No, she didn't."

Faith nodded slowly. "Oh, yes, she did. Trust me, that girl had a big thing for you."

"I never got that sense at all." He'd lived through the invitations to school dances being turned down. The indifference when he talked about the girls he dated. That lock being decisively thrust back at him.

"Kit wasn't like other girls," his mother added. "She probably went to great lengths to hide it, especially if she thought it wasn't reciprocated."

Holden lifted his feet from the railing and planted them on the ground. This conversation had taken an unexpected turn. It was hard to believe his family had picked up on this without him having a clue.

Buck winked. "Your mother has a sixth sense about these things."

She nudged Buck's foot with her elbow.

"Like it makes any difference now. I'm sure she's way beyond high school crushes." Faith waved her hand dismissively as she pushed away from the railing. "Buck, get that turkey out, please."

The conversation left him distracted. He missed half of the camaraderie swirling around the dinner table later that afternoon. Questions directed toward him were repeated, sometimes twice, before he snapped out of his Kit-fueled daze.

He wished he and Kit could have parted on better terms before the holiday, but she'd asked for time alone. The timing of the cleanup couldn't have happened at a worse time. She'd been resigned when he broke the news about the barge's arrival at Love's Landing. Quietly, he'd loaded the leftover food into his truck after that and drove off in the direction of home. He stood outside on his patio that night, watching her through her kitchen window. Her forehead rested on one hand while she held her phone in the other. With a sinking feeling, he'd known she was canceling her tours. That image of her had burned in his mind through the wee hours of the night, and it came to him at sporadic intervals since then.

"Holden."

His mother held a plate in one hand and a pie server in the other at the end of the table when he looked up. They'd caught him daydreaming again.

"Apple or pumpkin?" she asked, pointing to the two pies on the table. His father and grandparents were already digging in, their forks clinking against the Noritake china.

"Apple, please."

"Where are you tonight? Because it's certainly not here," she teased.

He smiled down at the plate she set in front of him and picked up his fork.

"Still unwinding from the hectic schedule up north, I guess."

"Maybe you should stick around a few days instead of heading back so soon," Nana said. "You're working too hard."

"I'd like to, but I need to wrap up the Port Chance project in the next week so I can be back here well before Christmas."

"He might as well stay in the rental as long as he can. An empty house is trouble," Buck said to his mother.

Nana finished the last of her dessert and set her fork across her plate.

"Maybe you'd like to stay there long-term?"

"In the rental? Nah."

Nana fixed him with one of her looks. "I mean Port Chance in general. You've always said it felt more like home than here."

"There's too much on my plate now before I can think about relocating." His mother must've shared the conversation about Kit from earlier. Nana's fondness for Kit had been unmatched when they were kids.

Later that night, after the others had left and his parents retired to bed, Holden propped himself against the headboard in the guest room and stared at his phone. He found Kit's number in his contacts.

One little tap and they'd connect.

What would he say?

More importantly, would she even want to hear from him?

Before he talked himself out of it, he called.

In the span of three seconds while the call connected, he almost hung up.

Then, when Kit's sleepy voice answered, he almost disconnected once more.

His mouth suddenly felt as dry as the cobble-strewn bottom of Huckleberry Creek.

"Hello?" she said again, irritation creeping into her tone. "Holden, are you there or not?"

"I am. How was Thanksgiving?"

"Crowded. Loud. But nice. How was yours?"

"Quiet, but nice, too. Nana said to tell you hello. Actually, everyone here did."

"That's...thank you."

Holden didn't know what he expected, but he got the feeling she wasn't in a talkative mood.

"Did I wake you?"

"No, just reading." There was a lengthy pause. "Why are you calling?"

He should have foreseen this. Talking on the phone just to pass the time wasn't Kit's way. He'd never called her just to shoot the breeze. And after what happened last week, awkwardness was the least he should've expected.

I wanted to hear your voice.

"I...ah...we'll be finished with the cleanup by Monday, Tuesday at the latest." He clamped down on his lips. Instead of a neutral topic to get the conversation flowing, he chose to bring *that* up? *Nice one, Holden.*

Another pause.

"You know, in case—"

"In case I want to reschedule the tours I had to cancel? Nope, too late for that. Those three groups made it perfectly clear they wouldn't be rescheduling anytime soon. Maybe never."

"But it wasn't your fault."

"It didn't make a difference."

He wanted to end the call before it hit a point of no return. Maybe it already had.

"I'm so sorry, Kit. How can I make it up to you?"

"You can make it up to me by staying far away from Love's Landing with your barge."

"I'm right in the middle of the cleanup."

"You asked. That's my answer." She sounded out of breath. "Nice article in the paper, by the way."

"Yeah?" He'd hoped she'd learn more about what EcoPartners was all about after reading it. Maybe she was even proud of him?

"I especially liked the part when you couldn't think of a single thing you'd miss about leaving town except Herrold's."

"I didn't mean it like that—"

"Or the part about loving your job because you're not tied down geographically. The nomad life suits you, huh?"

"Why is it important where I live? Weren't you a bit of a nomad at one point, too?" He chuckled, trying to keep it light. "What's the difference between you and me?"

"The difference is I'm not in my twenties anymore. I like being anchored to one spot, pardon the pun." Her tone reached such a fever pitch that she actually squeaked out the last few words. "But you're all over the place." Her voice trailed off.

"Kit, what do you need from me?"

"I need..." Her breath came out in a soft hush. "I don't know."

He stared at a distant spot on the opposite wall, trying to make sense of what Kit said. Was this all about him forcing her to cancel three tours? Or because he didn't have a home base? It didn't make sense. How could he fix this if he didn't know where to start? Kit didn't even seem willing to help him understand.

"I'm going to hang up. Maybe calling wasn't a good idea."

She swallowed noisily. "Okay."

And she beat him to it before he even said goodbye.

Chapter Twenty-Four

Holden stood on the deck of the *Dolly Swain* two days later, hoping he hadn't come back to Port Chance in vain. He wished for Kit to be standing here with him, but so far, she was nowhere to be found.

She'd left home that morning while it was still dark, her truck lights painting stripes on the wall through his bedroom blinds, and she hadn't returned by the time he was ready to head to the office.

His calls went unanswered.

He'd even driven out to Apple Hill Farm with the excuse that he needed a fresh cider donut from the farm store to start his day, but he hadn't spotted a single Wendell.

The parking lot at the landing, with a thin blanket of fresh snow, was void of tire tracks except his own.

Now, his boots echoed on the deck as he approached the wheelhouse of Kit's boat. It was locked up tight for the season, void of the personal touches Kit had kept at her side while she led tours. The insulated cup covered with random stickers, the

Bald Eagle bobblehead on the console, and the metal tin of peppermints were all gone.

He looked back at the parking area, hoping to see her truck pulling in. He'd even welcome a confrontation about what he was doing standing on her boat, not that he had a solid reason to offer.

No Kit.

A breeze ruffled his hair and crawled down the collar of his coat. He shivered, and moved closer to the wheelhouse to block the wind. A few hundred yards up river, EcoPartners' barge sat at the point near the state park. His crew and a dozen volunteers scurried around on the barge and along the shore, busy with the cleanup. He'd just come from there, dropping off two dozen donuts and coffees for a morale boost. Dan had even shown up to lend a hand after coming to town to house hunt with his wife. The crew raced against the weather report today; more snow was expected that afternoon. Holden planned to join them again later to hopefully wrap up the project until spring.

But first things first—he had to find Kit.

The abrupt end to the call the other night haunted him. She'd misunderstood what he'd told the newspaper reporter. There was so much more between those lines of black ink she'd read in the article. Whether she wanted to hear him out, whether she believed him or not, he'd try to explain himself. This time when he left town, there'd be nothing left unsaid. And there would be a proper goodbye.

He glanced at the parking lot again, hoping to see her truck sitting there, Kit scowling at him through the windshield. He smiled. Despite the heaviness in his chest, Kit—her taciturn moods and all—had blazed into his heart once again and lit his spirits on fire. Even if he didn't believe a word of what his mother claimed, Kit harboring some secret crush on him, the idea stirred inside of him.

If only that were true.

The bronze plaque on the wall beside the wheelhouse door caught his eye when his attention shifted away from the barge. He'd noticed it the day of his tour with the governor's office, but he'd quickly forgotten about it amid the commotion. Without distractions, he read it now.

Welcome to the *Dolly Swain*, a refurbished tug boat, which was put into service near the confluence of the Missouri and Mississippi Rivers in 2002. After spending two decades working with commercial traffic in southern Illinois, the tug journeyed north and was lovingly restored as a passenger ferry by Captain Kit Wendell and Stelling-Powers Boatworks.

A chuckle resonated in his chest.

Captain Kit Wendell.

Would there ever be a time when she didn't amaze him?

The *Dolly Swain* commemorates the *Dalliard*, a mid-19th century freighter commandeered by Captain John Holden. The captain and his wife, Dolly, lived near Burlington, Iowa, with their five children. He bestowed his wife's maiden name, Dalliard, on the boat before its first voyage in 1852.

Captain Holden.

Funny, she never mentioned the captain's name when they'd first talked about why she chose the name for her boat. He kept reading.

On April 14th, 1859, the *Dalliard* sank when she ran aground during a spring storm very near the same spot that the *Dolly Swain* was put into service. Although Captain Holden and his crew escaped to safety, the experience left the captain too disheartened to return to the river. The remains of the *Dalliard* eventually succumbed to the elements, and was buried for decades underneath silt and debris until she was discovered in a field along the river's flood plain.
The *Dolly Swain* pays homage to the beleaguered captain and his wife, and his boat, the *Dalliard*, whose life on the river was short-lived but fruitful.

Holden read the plaque again, barely able to contain his smile. Sharing a name with the captain who inspired her boat's moniker was more than a coincidence.

He thrust his hands deeper into his pockets when a gust swept across the deck. He eyed the plaque one last time before he made his way off the boat, heading toward his truck again.

Holden checked his phone once he was in the driver's seat.

No calls.

While he waited for the cab to warm, he let his mind wander over the last few months.

Port Chance didn't feel like the same place he left when he was eighteen. He'd been away too long. Strangers had moved into his boyhood home. His favorite tree had long been cut down to make room for a new shed. Businesses disappeared before new ones popped up like the women's boutique on Main Street, Daily Grind Coffeehouse, and Rose's new bakery.

The things he'd taken for granted—like the waves from passing strangers, the oak-shaded and meandering walkways of Larkspur State Park, and the Mississippi River as a backdrop to it all—brought about a newfound appreciation.

But then there were memories that also burned.

The sting of careless words.

Having a lock he'd painstakingly etched initials onto pushed back into his chest. Then watching Port Chance disappear in his rearview mirror weeks later.

Holden pulled away from Love's Landing, thinking about how he'd leave again soon.

He wouldn't make the same mistakes again.

On his way home, Holden drove down Main Street. Most businesses had already decorated for Christmas. He'd seen the posted signs advertising the annual holiday festival. Even Jumpin' John Goodwin's place was decked out.

On a whim, he pulled in next to Jumpin's Shoppe of Curious Goods. He hadn't seen the old man since he'd been back.

"If it isn't little Holdy Berne all growed up like a bean sprout," Jumpin' boomed in his gravelly voice as he ambled around his counter to greet him.

"It's been a minute, hasn't it?" Holden said as they exchanged a hearty handshake.

"A lifetime of minutes is more like it." Jumpin' clapped him on the back. "I heard you were back in town. How long are you staying?"

"I'm wrapping up the project now. I'll probably be out of everyone's hair in the few days."

Jumpin' asked about his family, and Holden showed him photos of his parents and grandparents. They reminisced about Jumpin's wife, who passed away years ago. She'd babysat Holden and his brother for a time.

"So did you come in just to say hi to an old man, or are you looking for something special?"

He didn't have anything in mind earlier, but now that Jumpin' mentioned it, yeah, there was something.

"Can I see what locks you have?"

Jumpin's eyes lit up. "Locks, eh?"

Holden nodded.

"Making plans, are you?"

Holden chuckled, feeling his cheeks warm. "Not really. I just want to see them."

"That's funny. Your friend came in not too long ago and asked me the same thing."

"Friend?" Now his face flamed. He knew whom Jumpin' referred to even before he said her name.

"Yeah, Ms. Kit. Went straight to the case," he said, hooking his finger at Holden to follow him.

"What for?"

"There's only one reason people show an interest in locks in this town," Jumpin' said.

He suddenly felt light on his feet, like he walked on a bank of clouds instead of the concrete floor. Why had Kit come to look at the locks? *Was it about me?*

Holden stopped in front of an old display case with four loaded shelves. There were dozens of locks. Some looked new.

Others were battered by time, rusty and scratched. He knelt to look at the bottom shelf. An iridescent green one caught his eye.

"Mind if I open it?" he asked, his hand on the sliding door.

"Not at all."

Holden pushed the door aside and reached into the case, plucking the lock from its resting spot on the length of pink velvet fabric. He turned it over to study both sides. It looked similar to the one he'd tried giving Kit. There were no initials, of course. Their lock was in the river, after all. He set it down again and stood.

"Nothing catch your fancy?" Jumpin' asked.

Holden bit the inside of his cheek. Jumpin' was studying him hard.

"Not this time, I'm afraid."

Jumpin' led him back down the aisle again to the front of his shop.

"You know where to come when it's time, don'tcha?"

"I do."

Holden left the shop almost breathless with questions swirling around in his head.

Was it possible that Kit had regrets? Maybe him coming back to town had dredged up these memories, and it'd taken her time to sort out her thoughts. He couldn't think of any other reason why Kit would come to Jumpin's shop solely to look at locks.

Maybe that was a question for him to ask Kit.

Chapter Twenty-Five

K it's yawn drew the attention of the barista named Merris behind the counter at Coffee Loft on the Monday following the long weekend.

"You're getting a triple shot this morning," Merris joked as she got to work on her order even before Kit said a word.

"Sorry, that was rude." Kit clapped a hand over her mouth as another yawn caught her by surprise. "Must be the snow. I just want to hibernate."

"I get it," Merris said. "Ginger should be down any minute. She's probably hibernating herself."

Kit had made her twice-weekly run out to the farm bakery before the sun came up to fetch the bakery order for Coffee Loft. Ginger kept the café's small case stocked with her own pastries, but no one did apple cider donuts better than Linn Miranelli and her staff at Apple Hill Farm. As a friend, Kit delivered them to Ginger's place and earned a complimentary pick-me-up as a trade-off.

Ginger appeared as Kit found her usual spot on a green velvet couch in the back corner of the café. She'd sit there, watching customers wander in, while she finished her coffee. Sometimes the café was too busy for Ginger to give her more than a wave and a few words when Kit brought in the donuts. Today, Ginger headed to the green couch, too, and sank into it next to Kit.

"Looks like you've already had a rough day." Dark shadows underneath Ginger's eyes told the story.

Ginger sighed. "Cal and I had our first real fight."

"Impossible."

"Sad, but true." She forced a smile. "It was silly. He commented about how I load the dishwasher. It'd been a hectic day, and I was feeling extra sensitive. I snapped at him. That unleashed a whole laundry list of what irritates us about the other."

"I'm sorry."

She waved it off. "We're better now. But we did stay on the phone until two this morning hashing it out."

"Hence the..." Kit motioned toward her own eyes.

"Exactly." Ginger paused. "So, your tour season is over, I hear?"

"It is. I had to cut it short by a few days, but I'm good."

She'd spent the day after Thanksgiving giving the *Dolly Swain* a good cleaning now that her supplies were stored away until early spring. Knowing Holden was out of town, she didn't have to worry about looking over her shoulder, wondering if he'd pop up unexpectedly.

"And your old friend, the guy who's leading the cleanup, was he apologetic?"

"I suppose." Kit blew air out of her cheeks. "I just wish he could have been more forthcoming about the whole thing and had given me a heads up before coming back to town."

"Maybe that's all the time he had," Ginger said. "That newspaper article about him and his company was an eye-opener. What a huge endeavor, cleaning up the river."

"It is." She hadn't seen the article until after Thanksgiving dinner, thank goodness, or her appetite would have been ruined. She'd found the newspaper lying on an end table in her parents' living room. Holden's grinning image against the backdrop of the barge on the river sent her heart into her throat.

"I can't imagine the hoops he jumped through to make it happen. Just securing the permits for my mobile coffee truck, my goodness, there was so much involved." Ginger leaned forward with excitement lighting her face. "Which, by the way, is going to make an appearance at the Christmas on the River Festival."

"Congratulations! I hope it's a great night for you," she said, her mind distracted about what Holden went through to organize the cleanup.

"Anyway," Ginger continued. "I hope you and him work through this."

"You're right. I just can't let it go for some reason."

Ginger stood and plumped the pillows on the couch.

"He obviously cares about you, or he wouldn't have involved you so much in the process to begin with."

Kit made a face but nodded.

Kit left Coffee Loft after saying goodbye, sipping her still-warm coffee as she followed the sidewalk down toward the next block where she'd parked.

Her thoughts drifted back to the night of the bonfire as she walked. What had she told Holden that night, that she didn't like the word "no"?

She'd thrown that word at Holden plenty since he'd come back to Port Chance.

No, I don't want you in my life.

No, I won't allow you to love me, even as a friend.

No, no, no, no.

She'd become her own worst enemy. She also realized that weariness had replaced the bitterness. Ever since Holden arrived back in town, she'd carried the burden of resentment around like an iron yoke. She was tired.

And now he'd be leaving soon. She'd been so busy trying to shove him out of her life again that she realized that she'd miss him when he left. *Really* miss him.

Kit stopped at the corner, waiting for the light to turn green again, all the while trying to avoid looking at the brick building across the street.

EcoPartners' offices were on the second floor.

Maybe it was the extra shot of espresso Merris added to her latte, but before she realized where her feet were taking her, she'd hoofed it across the street to the building's glass double doors.

Inside, she took the stairs two at a time, arriving in the second-floor lobby just outside Holden's office, out of breath and flustered.

What in holy bells are you doing here, Kit?

That thought was interrupted by a clatter and a curse inside the office.

Kit pulled open one of the double doors and froze.

Portia stood on top of the desk in her bare feet, reaching for the light panel above her head. The plastic covering came down on top of her head when it slipped through her hands. Her attempt to catch it resulted in a frenzied dance that almost landed her on the floor. Instead, the plastic panel hit the desk and knocked off a succulent in a white ceramic vase, which shattered. Portia cursed again, and that's when she noticed Kit standing there.

Kit offered a little wave. "Hi there."

Flush-faced and wide-eyed, Portia eased herself down into a kneeling position, no small feat for a woman her size, then slowly touched the floor. She smoothed her dress, rolled her shoulders, and gave her cinnamon bun up-do a little pat.

"Can I help you?" Portia said between her pursed lips.

Regaining her dignity took some work on Portia's part after the spectacle Kit just witnessed, but Kit had to hand it to her. It was a valiant effort.

"I'm looking for Holden," she said as she looked toward his darkened office.

"He won't be in until later," Portia said matter-of-factly.

"Okay..."

"Can I give him a message?" Portia asked curtly.

Kit wrinkled her nose.

"I'll just call him." Kit started to back toward the door but stopped. She pointed toward the ceiling. "What's going on up there?"

Portia slid her glasses to the top of her head and frowned. "The blinking from that light fixture is going to give me a seizure. I was trying to take the bulb out, but I can't reach it."

"Do you have spare bulbs?"

Portia nodded toward the back of the office. "There's a supply closet, but the building cleaning crew keeps it locked."

"Do you mind if I take a look?" Kit hooked her thumb toward the closet.

Portia gestured in that direction. "Like I said, it's locked, but be my guest."

The woman steered Kit toward the far end of the room. One glance at the doorknob told Kit she'd have it open in no time.

"Got a paper clip?"

Portia rummaged through the drawers of the nearest desk. She came back with one, which Kit quickly extended. Pressing one end into the tiny hole in the center of the knob, she gave the knob a few quick twists before the lock disengaged.

"Well, look at that," Portia said in wonder.

"My older sister liked to lock herself in her bedroom when we were kids. Our mother relied on me to get her out."

Portia nodded appreciatively.

Kit retrieved a replacement fluorescent bulb from the closet and spotted a ladder nearby.

"So you'll change it, too?" Portia asked.

"Faster than fall turns to winter on a northbound highway."

Portia grinned. It transformed her whole face.

It's probably a little like looking into a mirror.

She hadn't smiled much in Portia's presence either.

It took less than two minutes to pull out the defective bulb and install the new one.

"Thank you," Portia said. "You came along at the right time."

She chuckled. Kit—and probably Portia, too—couldn't have imagined uttering that sentiment the last time Kit stepped into the EcoPartners office.

"Holden will be happy to hear you stopped by," Portia said, settling back into her chair. "Don't be a stranger."

"I won't."

"Believe me, he's much easier to work with when you two are on good terms."

Kit waited for Portia's punchline, but the woman was as serious as a three-piece suit.

She affected Holden's moods? A surge of emotion rushed through her. What did that mean?

It was simple. He cared for her. At this point in her life, that was all she wanted from him. It was enough.

Outside, the snow came down in dense, fat flakes. The wind picked up, too, blowing the snow horizontally into her face. Yet despite the frigid air and the prospect for a snowstorm looming over the area, Kit pulled her parka hood over her head and dipped her nose into the collar of her coat, hiding a smile she could barely contain.

Chapter Twenty-Six

Projections of more than a foot of snow over the next twelve hours appeared on the weather app on Kit's phone. She shoveled her front walk twice before she called it a day. Plows appeared on the highway, their orange lights blinking as the only contrast against the white landscape. Inside, Kit fed logs into the wood stove, which warmed the little room with the big windows off her kitchen. It was her favorite room in the house because of the natural light, but it was also the coldest. She changed into sweatpants and her oversized Port Chance Pickles sweatshirt, feeling Holden's presence within its folds. She made some turmeric and ginger tea, then settled into the overstuffed chair that overlooked her backyard now covered with a solid white blanket in the waning daylight.

Her thoughts drifted like the snow.

Holden.

Their friendship. The memories. Starting now, she'd steer her mind away from the low points of their relationship and replace them with the good memories. The shared moments with their families. Their mutual love of baseball, the outdoors, and life on the river. It would be freeing to stop resenting Holden for the things he didn't feel and couldn't say to her. It'd certainly taken a village to get her to this point. Her family, Ginger, and—goodness—Portia, too. This mindset left her with a contentment that hugged her like the thick fleece throw tucked around her body. Even when Holden would eventually leave Port Chance, they could part ways on good terms. Knowing the road connecting them was free from bitterness left it open for the future, whatever that held.

Now, she just needed to share this with Holden.

A noise jolted her awake. She hadn't meant to doze off.

The light outside had changed, but not by much.

A bark. It sounded close to her deck.

Pushing the throw aside, she padded to the window in her slippers to peer outside.

The snow, heavier now, blurred the shapes in her yard. There was no movement except for the tree tops swaying under their burden of white.

She jumped when a snow-covered animal darted across her deck and disappeared at the corner of her house.

Sarge? He'd never come into her yard before.

Kit grabbed her coat from the mudroom and slipped into her boots. The deck door, half frozen with ice and the accumulation of snow, fought against her weight as she struggled to open it. A dusting of powder blew onto the floor before she was able to close it again from the outside.

Kit stood on the deck, scanning her yard. A few seconds later, the form dashed across her lawn toward Holden's, loping in a wide arc around the garden. It had to be Sarge.

She trudged closer to the railing and whistled. The dog froze, perking up its frosty ears, then resumed its crazed charge.

Holden was nowhere in sight, which was strange. He always kept a close eye on Sarge when he let him out.

Grumbling under her breath about mismanaged dogs and their owners, she high-stepped over to the hedge dividing the yards, and—

Holden was flat on his back near his patio, facing up toward the sky.

"Hey!" she shouted.

No response.

Is he injured? Having a medical emergency?

"Holden!"

She plodded through the drifts toward the opening in the hedge, then knelt beside his motionless figure.

Holden opened his eyes at the same time she spotted the wide swaths of snow pushed aside by his legs and arms.

Was he making—?

"Can't a guy make a snow angel in peace?"

He grinned as fat snowflakes dotted his reddened complexion. He sat up, tugging his ski cap farther down around his ears.

She gave him a hearty shove.

"You scared me. I thought you—"

Holden grinned. "Met an early demise? Nope. I just slipped trying to catch Sarge. Thought I'd have a little fun while I'm down here."

"Get up so I can push you back down." She stood and kicked a boot-sized pile of snow toward him.

When he got to his feet, Holden charged forward, gripping her around the waist to tug her down into the snow with him.

"What are you doing?" she screeched as she rolled away. Sarge, excited that others had joined in his hijinks, grabbed the hat from Holden's head and high-tailed it toward Kit's yard again.

Laughing, Kit brushed snow from her parka before it seeped into her collar.

"Sarge!" Holden called as he stood again.

The dog ignored him, bounding onto Kit's deck before he stopped to see if his game of keep-away was on or not.

"I'll get him," Holden said over his shoulder as he trudged toward her back door. "But I may need help."

Sarge must have sensed Holden meant business since he stayed put until Holden had him by the collar. Kit took Holden's hat out of the dog's mouth and fitted it over Holden's head again, barely keeping her laughter under control.

"It's always an adventure with him," he said.

"And with you as a neighbor." She loved how the cold had reddened his cheeks. The color of his eyes burned brighter, too.

"Sorry. Didn't mean to scare you." He grinned.

"Why don't you come in for a bit." Kit's heart hammered as she uttered the words. Until now, Kit wasn't sure she'd have the nerve.

"Sarge will melt all over your house."

"I have towels." She pulled the deck door open.

"Seriously, he does this thing when he comes in after being wet and cold, charging all over the house, jumping on the furniture..."

Kit shook her head. "It doesn't matter."

"Oh, you have no idea," Holden countered. "You have to see a Sarge tornado to believe it."

Now that she'd made up her mind, she wouldn't take no for an answer.

"I have something to show you."

Chapter Twenty-Seven

While he and Kit shed their boots and coats inside, Sarge gave the room a thorough inspection, leading with his nose. He didn't take off in a burst of fur, or jump on her furniture as predicted. Holden held his breath as Sarge circled the room, then explored the kitchen, the hallway, and the other rooms on the other side of the house. Soon he reappeared, casting a wide, doggy smile at Holden as if to say, "See? I can behave." Then the dog settled on the rug in front of the wood stove. Kit fetched a towel to dry him off, which Sarge contentedly allowed her to do, even turning over on his back so she could reach his underside. She giggled.

Holden looked up at the ceiling in disbelief.

"He's on his best behavior, believe me. This would never happen at home."

Kit rubbed Sarge's stomach. "Well, thank you for being a good guest, buddy." She stood. "Tea? Coffee?" she asked as she went into the kitchen to rummage in the cabinets.

"I'd love some."

While Kit filled a kettle with water, he wandered around the room, taking in the personal touches that filled her home.

The framed photo of her posing onboard the *Dolly Swain*.

A half-filled University of Iowa coffee mug.

Several issues of *Midwestern Life* magazine lay scattered across the coffee table.

A flier underneath one of the magazines drew his attention. He picked it up, smiling. It was the same one on display in Rose's bakery.

Fill a bag. Get a bag.

Kit's actions had always been more important than her words. Tuning out her brusqueness to see behind the facade was the challenge, though.

He held up the flier.

"I forgot to thank you for this."

"For what?" Kit asked, still focused on making tea. Steam escaped the kettle's spout.

"This was really...an amazing thing to do, Kit."

She looked up, squinting to see the flier from across the room. When she realized what it was, her expression changed. It was as if a shadow lifted, revealing another version of Kit.

She nodded and slowly removed the kettle from the stove before it began whistling. Kit turned off the burner, her movements hesitant. When Kit looked at him again, holding his gaze, the hair on his arms stood at attention.

Kit came around the counter and into the living room. She stared up at him, her brow furrowed.

"What's wrong? I wasn't going through your things. The flier was — "

"It's not that," she said.

"Then what?"

She took a deep breath. "I'm just going to get this out. You know me," she said. "Once I decide to...I can't..."

He nodded as a rush of adrenaline surged in his chest. *Talk to me.*

Kit swallowed. "Listen, I need to...um, *apologize.*" She wrinkled her nose when she spoke the last word as if it pained her to say it.

"What's up?" Was this about their phone conversation on Thanksgiving? She'd been short with him, though the call lasted no more than a minute.

"I'm sorry for not being a good friend," she said.

The blueness of her eyes had deepened. Standing this close, he marveled at the thick fringe of her lashes. Their effect made his mouth go dry.

"I haven't been for a very long time," she continued. "A good friend."

At her side, her hand flexed and curled. Holden desperately wanted to take it, to feel the softness of her skin again, the warmth inside his hand. Whatever this was about, it was hard for her.

"It's all right. Don't beat yourself up about it. I haven't been the most stellar friend either."

She frowned. "No, it was my fault we parted the way we did. I'd always hoped..."

So this wasn't about her chilly reception that day on the dock? Or her aloofness at the wedding last spring? She was reaching way back...

She shook her head, wincing. Whatever she intended to say, the struggle was ongoing.

Kit let out a groan. "Maybe it's easier to just show you."

She crossed the room to an antique mirrored cabinet that

also doubled as a fold-out desk. The desk, fully opened, revealed tiny drawers. Kit opened one. When she came back to him, her folded hands hid something.

"This might answer a lot of questions," she said, lifting her cupped hands closer to him.

At first, it looked like an ordinary lock. Short, silver shank. The brand name in a circle of blue in the center. But then he turned it over to the other side.

It was impossible. He'd imagined it on the bottom of the river, covered in layers of silt and rock. But the crudely etched initials and the date matched. This was the friendship lock he tried giving Kit senior year, the one she'd vehemently shoved back into his hands when she laid eyes on it. He'd pitched it into the water right in front of her. There'd been no harsh words after that. No follow-up apology phone call the next day. They simply didn't talk.

K.W. & H.B.

The BEST of friends, he'd carved into the matte finish.

When Holden looked up, he caught her staring, chewing on her lip. Her brows pinched so close together they almost looked attached.

"Where'd this come from?"

Even as the cold metal bit into the skin of his palm, he couldn't believe it. How could it be sitting in his hands if he'd thrown it in the river after Kit left him standing there next to the fence. Yet, he recognized his crudely shaped words.

"I found it," she said.

"In the...*river*?"

Kit nodded. The skin on her throat rippled as she swallowed.

"I saw you throw it. It took me days to find it in Pops' skiff.

His metal detector did the rest." She took a deep breath and let the air escape noisily.

"But...*why*?"

"I was mad." She shook her head, looking down, kicking at the floor. "Mad that you...thought we were friends. Mad that you left."

"What does that mean, that I thought we were friends?" He tried to connect the dots, to figure out what Kit was saying, but it didn't make any sense.

"I didn't feel important. Like I wasn't good enough to be... more."

He stopped breathing for a span of heartbeats.

Wait...*what*? He couldn't be hearing right. Her words spoke one truth, but he'd always believed another.

"You wanted to be *more* than friends?"

She nodded. When she spoke again, his knees almost buckled.

"Is it too late?" she asked.

Chapter Twenty-Eight

"*it.*"

The way Holden breathed her name, like it was a life preserver—like that one word would save him from drowning—made her hug her arms to her chest. The crazy-fast beat of her heart felt like it might leap from her chest.

"*Too late*? Are you asking me what I think it means?" he rasped.

Kit stepped back. *What kind of question is that*?

"I don't know how to ask it any clearer than that." She'd poured her soul into getting that out into the open.

He chuckled as he took her hands. "I'm not playing games. It's just...too good to be true."

She'd had enough of dodging the truth to last a lifetime. And what she heard from Holden was...that he had, too.

Her head swam.

Just say it.

But what if this was all in her imagination? Once the truth

was out there, she couldn't take it back. She could barely catch her breath to speak anyway.

Do it.

"I...I love you, Holden."

She wanted to close her eyes and wish away this moment if Holden didn't say something in the next few seconds.

A soft huff made her look up into his face.

His expression melted. There was no other word to describe it. He let out the tiniest of breaths before letting go of her hands. In an instant, he cupped her face and rested his forehead against hers.

"*Kit.* I love you, too. I always have."

His lips were like a whisper on her mouth at first. A soft brush, barely there, but it was enough that she grabbed his forearms in a sudden release of pent-up emotion. He leaned back to study her face as if to ask, *Is this okay?* When she pulled his arms toward her, the invitation was all he needed. Holden's lips met hers with a gentle kiss which slowly grew more urgent, leaving no doubt in her mind that he harbored the same desires. His arms encircled her, reeling her in against his chest where she could hardly catch a breath. Kit was determined that this kiss, this mind-numbing, soul-aching, delicious kiss would leave no doubt about the truth in her heart.

She'd hid it from Holden for far too long.

No more.

"I have to say it again," he said in a ragged breath against her lips. "I don't think I'll be able to stop saying it—I love you."

A gentle laugh tickled her throat. "Please don't stop. It's like a dream."

"This isn't a dream anymore. It's real," he said. His eyes were closed as he let the words flow from his mouth into hers.

Sometimes dreams do come true.

Chapter Twenty-Nine

She and Holden showed up the next weekend at Port Chance's Christmas on the River Festival holding hands. It caused such a stir that Kit thought their relationship status might outshine Santa's arrival in the vintage fire truck on Main Street. The first hint that it was big news came when they strolled past Jumpin's shop on the way to Ginger's mobile coffee truck.

"What's this holly jolly news that's buzzing on the street?" Jumpin' crowed from his perch on the front porch of his shop. The awning overhead was adorned with illuminated strings of snowflakes, another sign that Jumpin's frostiness had warmed with the holiday spirit. "My hearing aid must be on the fritz."

They stopped on the sidewalk.

"You've missed nothing," Holden said, squeezing her hand a little tighter. "It's all true. I'm living the dream."

Kit leaned into him, feeling the warm flush radiate throughout her body.

"Ah, young love. This does my rusty old heart good to see it," Jumpin' said. "It gives me hope for the world."

"Who told you this?" she asked.

"Your sister, of course. She stopped in, looking for something or another. Can't remember now," Jumpin' said as he scratched underneath his knit cap.

"Let me guess which sister. Janie?" she asked.

"She's the talker in your family, right?" His chuckle rumbled in his chest.

She and Holden wandered up the sidewalk after bidding goodbye to Jumpin'.

"I've forgotten how fast rumors can spread," Holden mused as they walked.

"Some people help more than others. Jumpin' is like the center of a wheel. All of its spokes lead to him."

"Did you tell your family?" Holden asked.

"No, I haven't."

"Then how would Janie know?"

"Janie specializes in snooping." Her sister had tracked her movements no doubt. Next time she had the chance, Kit would cut off Janie's ability to find her on that obnoxious phone app of hers.

She'd purposely kept their relationship status to herself, wanting to revel in the newness of her and Holden together without the outside noise. He'd awakened something in her that she'd never be able to live without now. It also didn't feel quite real yet. Shedding her fear that Holden might disappear again wouldn't go away overnight.

Holden draped an arm around her back and leaned his forehead against her head, seeming to read her mind.

"I'm not going anywhere, Kit. Please believe that."

She smiled up at him and gave him a firm nod.

They stopped to admire the blown-glass ornaments from

Blue Door Glassworks underneath one of a few dozen white tents of the artisans and food vendors lining the street. The aroma of roasted nuts and hot chocolate filled the air. A high school madrigals group stood next to the enormous lit Christmas tree, singing.

"This has really grown since I was last here in December," Holden said as he took the bag with the bubble-wrapped glass heart he'd bought for Nana from Rory Hilt, the glass artist.

"When were you here last in December?" She couldn't imagine him coming to town and not hearing about it.

"High school."

She snickered. "Then you've definitely been missing out."

"On many things," he said, stopping underneath a shadow-draped tree on the sidewalk. He pulled her against his chest. "And this most of all."

His lips were soft and warm despite the temperature. Kit closed her eyes, sinking into the perfection of his kiss as a well of emotion surged upward throughout her body.

So...this is what love feels like.

Her hand cupped the side of his face, feeling the heat of his breath on her skin. He tasted of chocolate and mint. Kit sighed.

Holden pulled away slightly, looking down at her with a half-smile. His hooded eyes smoldered.

"No complaints?" he whispered.

"Only when you stop." She pulled him closer again.

"Much more of this and we'll melt the snow under our feet," he murmured in a husky tone.

He was right. This would also add fuel to the rumor mill if anyone spotted them. Reluctantly, she gave him one more lingering kiss before taking his hand to resume their stroll down Main Street.

Up ahead, she spotted Travis and two of his buddies coming toward them. Her nephew looked pointedly at their interlocked hands and giggled into his coat collar. His friends did the same, the little copycats.

Kit hooked him around the shoulders before he could get away.

"What's so funny?" She put him in a headlock and knuckled his ball cap.

"Aunt Kit! No, owww!"

"Then tell me what you're laughing at."

Trav escaped her grip, red-faced and huffing. "Nothin'."

"There's definitely something. You're not a giggler." That made his friends laugh even harder.

The boy's glance darted between her and Holden, but he shook his head.

"Then get going and don't let me see your face again, or I'll knuckle you 'til you're bald," she teased.

"What was that about?" Holden asked as he watched Travis and his friends stumble down the sidewalk as they burst into laughter again.

"It's this." She raised their linked hands.

"Really? You'd think he's never seen a couple hold hands before."

"He has, just not his aunt Kit."

Holden looked down at her. "Never?"

"Nope," she said with a wink.

He laughed, shaking his head at her.

"I'm such an idiot for being so blind," he said.

"It wasn't all you. I share part of the blame. No one could have guessed my true feelings about you."

He pinned her with his gaze, smiling. "Not even yourself."

Someone whistled then, and it took Kit a few seconds to find the source. She pointed Holden to look across the street on the opposite sidewalk. A man waved as the woman and two children he was with tugged him along toward the line for the sleigh rides.

"Who's that?" she asked.

"My buddy Dan and his family," Holden said. "He'll be relocating here from Quincy in a few months. They're up here house-hunting again."

She couldn't see clearly with the number of people between them and the other side of the street. This Dan guy was still focused on them, holding his arms over his head.

"What's he doing?"

Holden squinted, laughed, then stuck his thumb up in the air.

"That's for us," Holden said, mimicking the heart sign Dan made with his hands.

"So, *you've* told people about us."

"Of course. Why wouldn't I? I love us." Holden pressed the back of her hand against his lips and gave it a noisy kiss through her glove.

"I love us, too. But I'm more of a keep-you-to-myself type, I guess."

"I've no complaints about that," he said, giving her hand an extra squeeze.

Ginger's coffee shop on wheels was parked outside of Rose's bakery. She and Holden waited for a lull in customers before they approached the window. Inside, Ginger and Merris hustled to clean and restock before the next wave of people came by.

"Hey, you two," Ginger said. Her smile was a wide as the mini camper she'd lovingly refurbished into Bark and Brew.

She'd committed to donating profits to a local shelter. "I've been waiting to officially meet your...*friend*."

Kit couldn't stifle the laugh at Ginger's poorly suppressed excitement.

"She's told me sooo much about you," Ginger said when she exited the truck and grabbed Holden's hand.

Kit huffed. "I have?"

"Oh, don't be coy," Ginger scolded. To Holden, she said, "She's talked about you nonstop. I feel like I've known you almost as long as she has."

Ginger exaggerated. Kit had dropped Holden's name over the last few weeks, but it wasn't like she *gushed* about him. That wasn't her, and Ginger knew it. Still, Holden liked hearing this, judging by his overly done grin.

Their small talk led them from the topic of Christmas plans to how long Holden might stay in Port Chance. Ginger over-shared about Kit's hopes that it might be indefinitely. Kit tried getting her to stop talking with a scowl, but Ginger ignored her. It was no secret, her wish that Holden might stay, but this was all so new and she didn't want to rush.

"You're the 'keep-me-to-yourself type,' huh?" he said with a wink after they left Ginger's truck, each with a hot chocolate in hand.

"I have my moments of weakness."

"You can be any type you want to be, as long as *I'm* your weakness." He sipped the hot chocolate, leaving a dark ring on his upper lip.

Kit stopped him on the sidewalk. "Here, let me."

She stood on her toes to kiss away the sweet spot.

"You as my weakness will never be a problem," she said.

Epilogue

(SEVEN MONTHS LATER)

On the first day of July, the *Dolly Swain* was at full capacity for the first time during her service at Love's Landing. There wasn't an inch to spare.

The entire Wendell clan had arrived first, clamoring out of their vehicles and down the pier as Kit readied the boat for a pre-Fourth-of-July sunset cruise up the river. Even Holden's parents, who were visiting for the long weekend, showed up. Holden remarked to her that it seemed like her family had grown by two since Buck and Faith Berne arrived. They fit right into the chaos of chatter and laughter.

"I brought snacks," Janie crowed as she hurried down the pier, holding up a foil-wrapped platter as Mark helped her aboard.

"And I have drinks," Rose said, lugging a cooler right behind her. She glanced around at the crowded deck. "This boat isn't going to sink with all of us on here, will it?"

"You'll be the first to go overboard if it starts," Janie teased over her shoulder. "Stop being such a worrywart."

Travis sacrificed his bench seat for Aaron and Sonya,

choosing to lean against the gunwale, but got shooed to an extra lawn chair by his aunt Sadie a minute later.

Inside the wheelhouse, Kit let the boat idle, warming it up for this epic, family-filled ride.

Holden came up behind her, draping an arm around her back.

"Why don't you come out here for a sec," he said.

"We're about ready to take off." She tapped the glass housing of the rpm monitor. It was still acting sluggish. "Can it wait?"

"I don't think so," he said.

With a sigh, she followed Holden out to the stern where everyone had grown strangely quiet. And they were looking at her.

"What's happening? Is there something wrong?" She tuned her ears to the sound of the idling engine. Was it rattling again? She'd meant to peek into the hatch on her day off, see if anything looked out of the ordinary.

Her mother pressed a hand against her throat, a habit Kit recognized when something worried her. "I heard a noise."

"Like from the boat? Where?"

"Maybe we should get off," Rose said, standing.

Everyone else stayed silent. Janie had clamped down on her lips so hard, they were barely visible. Next to Janie, Travis didn't look concerned at all. In fact, he seemed to be stifling a laugh.

"What's up with you? Spill it." Travis could never keep quiet. "Wait, what's up with *everyone*?"

"I think the noise came from back here," Holden said behind her.

When she turned, Holden smiled up at her as he balanced... *on one knee.*

She gasped.

"Holden."

He cupped a ring box in his palm with the lid open. A solitaire diamond ring resting on a bed of red velvet winked at her in the waning daylight.

"I know you're not crazy about surprises, and it's probably because you haven't had a lot of them since they're almost impossible with you...but I couldn't wait any longer." He took a breath, glancing around at their rapt, smiling audience, before fixing her with his gaze. "Kit, will you marry me?"

Their joyful whoops scared a flock of starlings from the treetops over their heads.

Holden stayed focused, waiting.

She tuned the others out, instead committing to memory the softness of his expression, the hope in his smile, and the endearing creases around his eyes. Did he already know how she'd answer? They hadn't talked about marriage at all, not that she wasn't willing.

A lump rose in her throat. She blinked away the blurriness as she looked down at the ring again. He'd asked her the one thing she'd dreamed about, even when she was too stubborn to admit it to herself.

Will you spend the rest of your life with me?

Her first attempt to answer him came out garbled. She giggled. Holden's smile was half relief, the other part pure delight.

"Yes. Yes, I'll marry you," she said, though this time she wasn't even sure if he heard her over the big collective "Yes!" from their families that resounded in her ears like a cheer. She laughed again as happiness bubbled inside her, and repeated her answer in case Holden didn't hear her amid the noisy celebration.

Holden stood to embrace her, hugging her so close she felt his heart beating through his T-shirt.

"How long have you had this planned?" she asked against his ear. Surprising her was no easy feat.

Holden tried to hide a smirk, but his twinkling eyes gave it away. "Since yesterday."

"Only since yesterday?" Holden was spontaneous, but how did that work for everyone else here?

"I figured the less time there was before I asked you to marry me, the better chance I had of pulling this off," he said with a shrug. "You know, with your reputation as a surprise killer and all."

"I'm amazed you were able to round everyone up."

He chuckled. "There was some rescheduling of plans, I was told. No one wanted to miss the proposal of the century, though."

His gaze aligned with hers. She shook her head. How could she question his intentions when Holden looked at her like that?

Their families came forward individually to congratulate them and share hugs. Kit was sure all of Port Chance could hear the ruckus at Love's Landing.

"This must mean you'll be sticking around Port Chance for a while?" Janie asked Holden, offering them a platter filled with Cupid's heart cookies to mark the occasion. "Wait, you're not going to steal my sister away, are you?"

"I think it's safe to say I'll be calling Port Chance home rather than asking Kit to leave here for somewhere else," he said.

That appeased Janie who squeezed Kit's shoulder with her free hand before she passed out more cookies.

It'd been a running joke since Christmas when they opened up about their true feelings. Holden hadn't left town for more than a few days each month since then. His EcoPartners crew had officially completed the cleanup two weeks ago. He'd oversee the new project ten miles up the river near Dubuque before heading south again for work on the Missouri in August. Amidst the comings and goings of his crew, he'd maintained the office in downtown Greenhaven, renting the space indefinitely. He'd assured her that he could work from anywhere. *I'm very portable*, he'd said.

Holden left her shortly after his parents, who couldn't contain their excitement over the happy news, joined them when Janie moved on. Kit had always loved Buck and Faith since they referred to her as the daughter they never had. She'd sat at their table for Sunday-night dinners more times than she could count.

Kit found Holden a few minutes later in the wheelhouse standing over the control panel.

"I'm pretty sure your mom just volunteered your brother's baby to be our flower girl."

Holden snorted. "She's not even born yet. And I don't want to wait that long."

"I didn't point that out since they're so excited." She paused. "What are you doing?"

"You're not the only one who knows how to steer a boat. Let's get this ride going, so I can have you all to myself later on."

A shiver rippled up her back. She wasn't going to argue.

"It looks good on you," he said, nodding to her left hand as she flipped on the depth finder. "You're not hard to shop for."

She splayed her fingers to look at the ring. It was perfect. Not flashy at all. Simple and uncomplicated. Holden knew her style. She pressed against his side, hugging his arm.

"You've always known me better than I know myself."

"Not always," he said, easing the throttle forward. The boat glided toward the sunset. "There are seventeen missing years to back up that fact."

They'd make up for time lost. They'd build a life together with a foundation of truth and love. She was going to marry Holden Berne, as incredulous as it seemed.

"But," he continued as he pulled her against his side, nuzzling her temple, "we have the rest of our lives to make up for it."

A Special Note to Readers

Thank you so much for reading *Locked on Love's Landing*. I hope you loved Kit's and Holden's love story as much as I enjoyed writing it. There's a prequel story to the series, *French Toast with a Side of Love*, that you'll enjoy for free if you join my newsletter Welcome to the Sweet Life. You'll also get access to other free content as well as subscriber-only giveaways, sneak peeks at new stories, and exclusive contests.

And, of course, if you enjoyed Locked on Love's Landing, I'd so appreciate you leaving a review on Amazon and/or Goodreads!

Happy Reading!

Dawn

Acknowledgments

- Thanks to Marisa Figueiredo for her insight while I wrote Locked on Love's Landing. Sickness set me back a few weeks, so her patience and flexibility didn't go unnoticed. Her expertise for helping me fix my mess of a manuscript is so appreciated.
- Thank you to my editor Sarah West who is such a pleasure to work with on this series.
- Many thanks to Mary Ellen Cox for being the last pass person to read through the manuscript, and also to Rachael Bloome for offering her wonderful words of wisdom on the early chapters.
- Thank you to Wilette Cruz for the beautiful cover. I wish Love's Landing was a real place, based on this stunning cover.
- Thanks to Gari Jean Sayles for suggesting Bark and Brew for the mobile coffee truck's name.
- Finally, much love to my family for your support and devotion.

About the Author

D.E. Malone writes contemporary small-town romance and is the author of the Hearts in Hendricks, Blueberry Point Romance, and Port Chance series. Her work has appeared in the Chicken Soup for the Soul series, *Highlights for Children*, and other publications. When not writing, she loves outdoors—gardening, hiking, and exploring places off-the-beaten path. She lives in central Illinois with her husband.